"If anyone leaves, it will be you!"

Zachary laughed shortly with amusement and contempt at Alisa's enraged expression. "But then you can't leave, can you, Mrs. Stuart?" he added tauntingly. "Not unless you want to give up Christine."

Alisa struggled to control her temper. "I paid a high price to marry you so that I could maintain custody of my sister." Her voice became sweetly sarcastic. "Therefore, I wouldn't dream of leaving you, my dear husband."

In her heart, she really longed to escape the torment of her marriage. But she loved Christine. Keeping her was worth the sacrifice she had made. It was worth living with a man who didn't care for her—even while she knew that he was having an affair with another woman!

JANET DAILEY AMERICANA

Every novel in this collection is your passport to a romantic tour of the United States through time-honored favorites by America's First Lady of romance fiction. Each of the fifty novels is set in a different state, researched by Janet and her husband, Bill. For the Daileys it was an odyssey of discovery. For you, it's the journey of a lifetime.

Janet Dailey Americana

ALABAMA—Dangerous Masquerade
ALASKA—Northern Magic
ARIZONA—Sonora Sundown
ARKANSAS—Valley of the Vapours
CALIFORNIA—Fire and Ice
COLORADO—After the Storm

These books may be available at your local bookseller.

Don't miss any of our special offers. Write to us at the following address for information on our newest releases.

Harlequin Reader Service
901 Fuhrmann Blvd., P.O. Box 1397, Buffalo, NY 14240
Canadian address: P.O. Box 603,
Fort Erie, Ont. L2A 9Z9

FIRE AND ICE

Harlequin Books

TORONTO • NEW YORK • LONDON
AMSTERDAM • PARIS • SYDNEY • HAMBURG
STOCKHOLM • ATHENS • TOKYO • MILAN

The state flower depicted on the cover is golden poppy.

Janet Dailey Americana edition published August 1986
ISBN 373-89805-3

Harlequin Presents edition published July 1976
Second printing March 1979
Third printing April 1981

Original hardcover edition published in 1975
by Mills & Boon Limited

CHAPTER ONE

'WITH your face and figure, you would have no difficulty getting a husband. Too bad you were born with such a frigid nature.' The young man leaned back in the chaise-longue along the plush Las Vegas hotel pool. He inhaled deeply on his cigarette while studying the golden tanned body of the girl sunbathing beside him.

'You forgot to add "and my money", Michael.' Her eyes remained closed, shutting out the glare of the Nevada sun midway down in the afternoon sky. 'And I wasn't born with a frigid nature. It took years of hard work before I successfully discovered its benefits.'

His gaze travelled over her slim ankles and the slender long legs, the soft lime-green two-piece swimsuit that accented her narrow waist and the gentle swell of her breasts, before stopping at her face to investigate the Grecian perfection of her profile and the pale gold colour of her naturally blonde hair. An amused chuckle escaped his lips, bringing one eye open to stare at him quizzically.

'My poor Alisa,' Michael stared at his cigarette rather than meet the cool gaze of her clear blue eyes. 'To be so hardened against men and yet placed in the position of having to marry one!'

'I see nothing amusing in that!' Alisa Franklin rose from her reclining position to reach out angrily to her gold cigarette case lying on the table beside Michael.

'Oh, come now.' A cynical gleam brightened his eyes as he leaned over to light her cigarette. 'Surely you see the twisted humour of the hand reaching out from the grave, especially when you consider it's all your mother's doing.'

'My mother was an intensely old-fashioned woman who believed that a woman wasn't complete without a man!'

'And managed to marry five times to prove it!' Michael laughed. His lean body, clad only in black trunks, leaned back against the chair.

'She was a fool!' Alisa exclaimed. 'A weak-willed person who hung on every man's coat tails, a simpering idiot with her lavender scents and lace handkerchiefs. She knew how I loathed those summers I spent with Roy and Marguerite – and she had the simpleness to be taken in by their snivellings and state in her will that they were to have custody of Christine!'

'Not to mention all that money that goes with her,' Michael added.

'I don't care a snap for the money and you know it.' She ground the half-smoked cigarette out in the ashtray. 'Mother knew my father's trust fund left me amply provided, which was the reason Christine was the main beneficiary of her will. The poor child will never enjoy any of it with Marguerite and Roy in control. You should have seen the way she looked at me when I left her there yesterday. Damn it! What am I going to do?'

'I don't see what you're getting so excited about,' he mocked. 'Your mother stated very clearly in her will that *if* you were married, the custody of Christine would be yours. You merely have to marry someone.'

She longed to cry out 'Never!', but the memory of Christine's pleading eyes danced in front of her face, making such a statement impossible.

'You forgot the provision that also states I must live with my husband for at least one year.' Alisa lit another cigarette and puffed on it in angry frustration. 'If only you weren't my cousin, you would solve all my problems. As it stands, I can't think of one man I'd like to spend an evening with, let alone twelve months!'

'The only reason you tolerate me is because I don't pander your ego as everyone else does.' Michael's mouth curled sardonically. 'I knew you when you had braces on your teeth and were as skinny as a reed, tagging along after me like a puppydog. I suppose your cynicism amuses me, as well as your money.'

'Don't try to sneer at me, Michael,' Alisa returned in a dangerously cold and quiet voice. 'You're only twenty-six, just two years older than I. You are an adequate escort, very occasionally amusing company, but more importantly, you don't subject me to those degrading pawing sessions.'

'The ice maiden has no cousinly affection for me at all? Perhaps you should seek a husband. He might be more satisfactory. I'd love to see you married to some domineering tyrant who would beat you twice a day.'

'You can wipe that smug smile off your face, because I'll never marry anyone that I can't succeed in having the upper hand with!' Alisa rose from her chair, sweeping her long white-gold locks away from her face before

7

slipping on the lacy beach robe. 'You did reserve a table for the Parisian revue this evening as I told you to do, didn't you? Or did you spend the money on the dice tables like you have all the rest I've given you since we came to Las Vegas?'

'No, I obeyed Your Highness's command and slipped an extra tip to the reservation clerk to ensure a satisfactory table.' He got to his feet, his slender tall frame giving him only a three-inch advantage as he stood facing her. 'I'll pick you up at eight-thirty. We'll have time for dinner before the eleven o'clock show.' As Alisa turned to leave, Michael asked quietly, 'What are you going to do about Christine?'

'Find a husband.' Her voice was sharp and contemptuous. But as she continued, Michael heard the ringing pride creep through. 'He'll be someone of quality with a respectable family name. I'll not marry some fortune-hunting scum and endure the laughter that would follow. Not even for my sister!'

Alisa didn't wait for Michael to comment on her statement. She traversed the full length of the pool area, disdainful of the ogling eyes and suggestive voices that followed her. Her total disregard to the male attention served as a spur to goad them to more attempts to gain her interest, but Alisa's disinterest was genuine. Her only reaction was one of revulsion that left an unclean feeling when she finally reached her suite.

Only after Alisa had been immersed in the marble bath filled with bubbling suds did she feel free of the disgusting traces of leering eyes. With an enormous white bath towel draped around her, she sat down in front of the vanity, gazing silently and absently at her composed reflection in the mirror. She had become accustomed to the perfection that stared back. Only once had Alisa wished she had been born a 'plain Jane', but that had quickly passed. Her own love of beautiful things would have rejected the lack of it in her own appearance, just as she realized, with insight, that had she been a plain girl, she would quite likely have possessed a romantically foolish nature, mooning and sighing over some man like so many of her other acquaintances did.

Now those silly notions were behind her, successfully buried with the braces and the gaucheness of waiting until her body had matured enough to catch up with her gangling long legs. With an amused and bitter smile, Alisa realized how much gratitude she owed her mother. Her mother had divorced Alisa's father, her first husband, only three years after the birth of their only child, Alisa. Two years later, when she was nearly five, he was killed in a car crash. She had clung childishly to his image, bestowing on him all the attributes that she dreamed a father would have. But the parade of men through her mother's life had quickly tarnished her faith. It had seemed to Alisa that she was forever being shuttled off to her Aunt Marguerite and Uncle Roy's to make way for another honeymoon or another divorce.

The summer of her fifteenth birthday had been the most traumatic of all. Her third stepfather, wealthy as all her mother's husbands were, had taken an intense interest in Alisa. The soft curves of womanhood had just begun to show on her previously slender boyish frame. The slight straightening of her teeth had been accomplished by braces and the unsightly wires were gone. For a month Alisa had basked in the warm glow of his attention. They had gone sailing together nearly every day. Her mother, who was a terrible sailor, had remained ashore. It was on one of those expeditions that Alisa had become aware of a change in his attention.

It was a gorgeously sunlit day, encouraging lazy hours spent sunbathing on the deck. The slight breeze had died, leaving the sails becalmed underneath the warm rays of the sun. Alisa had lain stretched out on the sailboat's deck, her simple two-piece swimsuit of the summer before not quite fitting her newly formed curves. She remembered her stepfather walking towards her, stopping to stare down at her. She remembered being puzzled by his gaze and the curious light that was in his eyes. A strange fear had swept over her when Alisa remembered they were alone on the boat and at least two miles from shore. She had shaded her eyes from the brilliant sun to gaze up at him, noticing for the first time the dissipated lines around his mouth, the paunch that showed quite visibly in swimming trunks, and the seemingly always constant can of beer in his hand.

He had knelt down beside her, his eyes resting on the slight cleavage of her swimsuit top before moving to the tiny pale gold topknot of hair on her head.

'Take your hair down, Alisa,' he had commanded thickly.

Her fingers had fumbled to obey as a shiver of fear raced through her. As her hair had cascaded down on to her shoulders, her stepfather's hand had reached out to capture the spun gold in his hands. Aware that what was happening wasn't right, Alisa had attempted to stand, but he quickly pinned her to the deck, his heavy breathing sending waves of alcoholic odour over her face as she tried to turn away.

'How about a kiss for your old stepdad?' he had muttered.

Kicking, scratching, and screaming, Alisa had tried to ward him off, but without much success as he at last had covered her mouth with his. The disgustingly repulsive memory of his mouth practically slobbering over her face was as fresh today as it was that afternoon when she had finally broke free and dived over the side. Luckily she had managed to flag down a passing boat which took her to shore, where she had sobbed out the story to her horrified mother.

Not even her mother's divorce and subsequent successful marriage to Dale Patterson had managed to erase or blot out the events of that afternoon. The beginnings of her cool reserve had begun. In the later years of her teens, Alisa was aware her looks were the envy of girl friends and that any of the more sought-after boys were hers for the asking. But few boys interested her enough, and those that did had always met the same fate. Alisa had realized with growing disgust that once you accepted a date with a boy, it wasn't the pleasure of your company that they were interested in. At first she had tried to endure the goodnight kisses, but they always expected more the next time. Gradually she refused all dates, hating the sense of obligation that came with the acceptance. She shunned nearly every social gathering, and those she couldn't, she was escorted to by her cousin Michael.

There were only two things she enjoyed out of life any more, her precocious half-sister Christine and the gaming tables in Las Vegas. Alisa's gambling wasn't an obsession; if she won, she stopped. If she was getting behind, she stopped too, always knowing that as long as her inheritance held out, there was always another day. But Christine? Alisa sighed deeply, removing a brush from the table, and began brushing her hair. There was no question about whether or not she wanted Christine.

Dear, darling little Christine whom Alisa had taken care of since Chris was a baby. To have Christine Alisa must have a husband, an incredibly simple solution for someone as beautiful and wealthy as she, but a terribly galling one at the same time. Even as names and faces danced in her head, Alisa was rejecting them. Never once did she doubt that if she chose one, she would fail to succeed in getting him to the altar. She loathed the more acceptable ones who were quick to cater to her just as she feared the ones who would attempt to force themselves on her. If only she could go out and buy herself a husband, Alisa thought with a smile, how simple it would be!

Although the entire revue had been well staged from the choreography of the scantily clad dancers to the individual acts of the entertainers, Alisa hadn't been able to enjoy the show. Her mind was centred on finding a solution to her problem. When Michael had picked her up earlier in the evening, Alisa had been determined to put her thoughts behind her, taking enormous time choosing her dress before finally settling on a new silver lamé evening gown, sleeveless and curling around her neck with a mandarin collar. With it she had worn a black lace shawl with silver threads running through the rose design. Her pale yellow hair she had styled to wing down the sides of her face from its centre parting to sweep back into a sophisticated chignon at the nape of her neck.

As they entered the casino area, Michael paused near the dice tables, a feverish gleam lighting his eyes as he watched the dice bounce across the green top. Poor Michael, Alisa thought without any sympathy. He had run through his inheritance in less than a year, but still he was anxious to lose more at the tables. She touched his elbow lightly and reluctantly he followed her as she continued wandering through the crowds.

The din of ecstatic winners and disgruntled losers mingled with the jangling bells of the slot machines and the casual voices of croupiers and dealers. People in expensive evening clothes rubbed elbows with others dressed in sporty wear. It was an incongruous mixture amidst the plush carpeting and dazzling chandeliers. There seemed to be only one place where the élite were separated from the average populace, and Alisa knew that her casual pace would eventually bring her to the secluded baccarat table.

Stopping at the ornate railing that isolated the players from the crowded casino floor, Alisa experienced again the tightening of her throat that always happened to her as she was about to take part in this aristocratic game of chance. Michael stood silently by her side, watching the coolness of her expression with the same amazement he felt every time they went through this routine. In a moment she would turn to him, discreetly pass him some money so that he could go off to his own game at the dice tables.

Through large, unexpressive blue eyes, Alisa studied the play in progress and the players. As her gaze drifted around to each person, she ignored the younger women at the table, seated there under the employment of the casino to add colour and inducement to legitimate players. Her pulse quickened as her eyes rested on the last player at the table.

His ebony black hair gleamed under the soft glow of the chandelier. Under the dark eyebrows, thick dark spikes of black lashes outlined his eyes, so dark brown that they appeared black. Even now, at this distance, Alisa could see the burning intensity of his gaze as he studied the cards before him. His tanned cheekbones sat prominently in his face, suggesting leanness that wasn't there. The long, narrow nose looked as uncompromising as the rest of him. Finally her eyes rested on the cruel line of his mouth.

Her left eyebrow lifted with her mounting excitement. There couldn't be two people who looked so much alike. A cool wave of resolution washed over her as Alisa turned slightly towards her cousin.

'That man sitting to the left of the croupier, what do you know about him?'

Michael glanced at her in surprise. Alisa was usually unconcerned about who she played with and rarely showed any interest in her fellow players, but obediently his gaze went to the man in question. As he recognized the man, Michael inhaled deeply to conceal his surprise. When he turned to Alisa he was equally surprised to see a glittering light in her eyes.

'That's Zachary Stuart. I haven't seen him in Vegas since before his father died. He's a ruthless gambler, or at least, he was. He had the most uncanny luck at the tables, especially when you consider that he never seemed to care one way or the other. You'd do well to follow his lead in betting, Alisa.'

'I don't care how he gambles.' Her gaze returned to the man at the table with a chilling calculation in her expression. 'I want to know everything you know about him.'

'What for?' But at the freezing flash of her blue eyes, Michael shrugged his resignation. 'You probably know as much as I do. I'm sure you've seen him at a couple of Elizabeth's parties in San Francisco. His father was a big import-export tycoon in San Francisco, dabbling in real estate and land developments. He went under about seven years ago when he invested a little too heavily in a development that was wiped out by mud slides. Rumour had it that the accident that killed him was really suicide, but it was never proved. Zachary — he was about twenty-five at the time — inherited all the debts, which is about the time he stopped coming to Vegas. I've heard that the only thing that he was able to keep, outside of his mother's house in San Francisco, was a small vineyard in Napa Valley. The winery and the vineyards had been abandoned for several years, so I understand, which means the slim profits he has made these last few years have been poured back into the property.'

Alisa permitted herself a smug smile when Michael finished. 'So the arrogant Mr. Zachary Stuart is in need of money,' she thought with jubilant bitterness.

'He looks like a man who would do anything for money,' she commented aloud.

'I don't know if I would put it quite that way. Let's just say he would be pretty ruthless in getting what he wanted.'

'Is he married?'

'Him? No. Does he look like the marrying kind? Though there've been an ample number of women who've tried.' Michael laughed softly as he withdrew a cigarette from his pocket. 'He has a similar view of women to what you do of men, with the exception that he believes women were put on earth for the purpose of providing a sexual outlet for men. I'm sure it's quite rare for him to find a woman who would deny him his pleasure.' He glanced at Alisa with mocking amusement until he saw the grim, calculating expression on her face. 'Oh, no, Alisa, if you're thinking what I think you're thinking, you'd better just forget it. There's one man that you couldn't make toe the line.'

For half a second, Alisa felt a twinge of fear that Michael could just be right, but she quickly pushed such a thought aside. 'He meets all the requirements: a respectable family name though a little impoverished, and a person of breeding. It's all a matter of price, Michael dear.'

'You might consider how much you'll have to pay,' Michael said, but Alisa ignored him as she walked forward to the roped gate, nodding serenely to one of the men when he escorted her in and seated her at the baccarat table beside Zachary Stuart.

Although Alisa received several appreciative glances from other male players, there was no such recognition coming from Zachary Stuart. She sensed his indifference to her and set about subtly drawing his attention to her. At first she waited to place her bet until he had done so, then deliberately bet opposite him. He played exceedingly skilfully with Lady Luck sitting on his lap. Still he seemed unmoved by the growing stack of money in front of him and totally oblivious to Alisa's bets. Finally she removed a cigarette from her case, tapped it lightly on the table, and let it dangle in front of him absently as she watched the play. But when he courteously offered her a light, she declined and placed the cigarette back in its case. A few minutes later Alisa removed the cigarette again and just as Zachary's hand came out of his jacket pocket with a lighter, she turned to an older man on her other side and asked for a light. The deliberate affront successfully brought Zachary's attention to her.

When he refused his turn to deal the cards from the shoe, Alisa did likewise. The small stake that she had started off with was nearly depleted, so she abstained from placing any bet. As she leaned against the back of the chair, she felt his dark gaze studying her. Now she turned to meet it, her own eyes sparkling with the excitement of this new game she was playing.

"Would you like to have a drink with me?" he asked in a low, well modulated voice that had a condescending ring to it, even as the dark fire of his gaze mocked her.

'I don't know you,' Alisa replied coolly, reaching

forward to stub her cigarette out in one graceful movement.

'That's easily remedied. I'm Zachary Stuart.' He indicated to the banker that they would be cashing in.

'Alisa.... Alisa Franklin,' she said calmly, despite the quivering elation of triumph racing through her as he rose to pull out her chair for her.

Without inquiring her preference, Zachary Stuart proceeded to guide her towards one of the quieter, more secluded, dimly lit lounges on the edge of the casino floor. She discovered that he was uncomfortably taller than she. When Alisa was wearing heels, she was nearly five foot ten, which usually put any of her dates at eye level. But with Zachary Stuart, she just reached his chin. His height also gave the illusion of slenderness that was extremely misleading, for the breadth of his shoulders was very intimidating. Alisa was glad when they were finally seated at a small table and she no longer had to look at him.

He ordered two dry Martinis, again without asking her preference, which she found quite irritating. With anyone else and in any other circumstances, Alisa would have refused the drink when it arrived at the table, merely to assert her authority since on her own she probably would have ordered the same drink. In this case, she managed to accept it graciously and quelled the tiny rebellion inside. As Alisa took a cigarette from her case and placed the filter-tipped end to her lips, a lighter snapped open and touched its yellow-orange flame to the cigarette.

'Tell me,' Zachary Stuart said, 'are you always like that?'

'I beg your pardon?' Alisa nearly choked on the smoke.

'About who lights your cigarettes? That was a very ingenious and insulting way to get my attention, but then you succeeded very completely.' His face was shadowed, but his voice left no doubt that he was amused by her ploy. 'Alisa Franklin. I believe I've heard your name before.'

'It's quite possible. My mother, Eleanor Patterson, was killed in a plane crash a few weeks ago.'

'I can see you're in deep mourning for her.' His sarcasm brought a chilling coldness to her face which she quickly tried to hide.

'I believe I've heard of you before, too, Mr. Stuart. Wasn't your father a quite important person in San Francisco before his . . .' Alisa paused so that her words would carry the full implication, '. . . untimely death. You have a small vineyard now, I believe, in Napa Valley.'

'You seem to know a great deal about me.'

'Just bits and pieces,' Alisa replied with biting softness. 'How's business?'

Zachary leaned forward, the small candle on the table illuminating his face and giving a sardonic curl to his lips.

'I have the strange feeling that if I said it was good you'd be disappointed.' He regarded her with malicious amusement as a fleeting expression of discomfort flashed across her face. 'You seem a little too frostbitten to want the key to my hotel room, so why don't you tell me exactly why you agreed to have a drink with me?'

'You're quite right. I dislike wasting time with subtilities. I have a proposition to make to you, Mr. Stuart.' At the disbelieving arched eyebrow, Alisa added hastily, 'A business proposition.'

When she paused for his reaction, Zachary moved back into the shadows of the lounge. Alisa tried to stifle the growing irritation, but some of the sharpness crept through.

'I understand that you are a little financially strapped right now, that you could use some money to make improvements on your vineyard and winery. I am prepared to give you that money.'

'That's very interesting. I can't help wondering why you should choose my business to invest in. Surely there is something you hope I will give you in return.'

The barest hint of colour touched her cheeks as Alisa straightened her shoulders and lifted her chin and spoke with as much dignity as she could.

'I need a husband.'

A short, derisive laugh came from the man across the table. 'There must be any number of marriage-minded men who would jump at the chance to marry a beautiful woman such as yourself. I recall hearing your name linked with Paul Andrews. Why don't you marry him?'

'Paul?' For a brief moment, Alisa groped to put a face to the name, before the image of a strong, gentle man with light brown, almost blond hair was brought to mind. 'He was a silly little milksop who panted at my

20

heels like a puppydog. The palms of his hands were always sweaty.' Alisa's voice was quite expressive in her distaste, although her expression remained composed and indifferent.

'Did you hear he attempted suicide when you ordered him to leave you alone? It was about a year ago, I think.'

'That was a feeble-minded and spineless thing to do. Undoubtedly he couldn't succeed at that either.' Paul Andrews was a tiresome subject to Alisa, one that was taking their conversation away from the business at hand. 'My marriage would only be temporary. That's why I'd prefer it to be to a stranger.'

'Are you pregnant?'

'Of course not!' Alisa denied vehemently and angrily.

'Well, it is the usual reason why most women have to get married,' Zachary mocked, his dark eyes twinkling at her in amusement. 'What do you have to gain by marriage?'

'My half-sister Christine, who's seven years old,' Alisa retorted in cold defiance, wishing she could slap that derisive and sarcastic expression from his face. 'My mother's will stated that I could have permanent custody of Christine only if I was married and had lived with my husband for one entire year. Otherwise her guardianship would go to my aunt and uncle.'

'Do you care for this little girl, or do you just hate your aunt and uncle?'

'My feelings for both are equally intense – if it's any of your business.' She lifted the Martini glass to her mouth and sipped it calmly.

'If I were to agree to your ridiculous proposal, what would you be prepared to pay me?' The lighter flared again in the dimly lit room as Zachary inhaled on his cigarette. The brief, flickering flame revealed black fires in his eyes as he watched her reaction.

'It would depend on what you required.'

'Around two hundred thousand would adequately take care of the modernization,' he replied.

'You're a very high-priced person.' The words were drawn through tightly clenched teeth which managed to prevent Alisa from telling him exactly what she thought.

'You get what you pay for, Alisa. My freedom is worth a great deal to me.' He studied the smoke from his cigarette, it grey trail drifting lazily near his face. 'What made you decide to put your proposition to me?'

It had been at one of Elizabeth's parties, just as Michael had said, when Alisa had seen Zachary Stuart. Paul Andrews had been making himself a persistent nuisance. Perhaps that was why when he had left her side to greet the tall, dark-haired man just arriving, Alisa had spared the time to look. It had been Zachary Stuart, Alisa realized now. Paul had attempted to bring Zachary over to introduce him to Alisa, but Zachary had declined.

Later in the evening when Alisa was just leaving the ladies' powder room, she had overheard Zachary talking. It had been a case of accidental eavesdropping, with only his profile against a backdrop of greenery to

22

identify him. But he wasn't the kind of man one would forget.

Some woman had been teasing him about his reluctance to meet Paul's new love. Zachary Stuart's cutting reply had remained with Alisa.

'From what Paul has told me,' Zachary had said, 'she isn't my type of woman.' He had spoken with the cool arrogance of a man who always got what he wanted. 'I wouldn't waste my time on some cold, dumb blonde who would be afraid a man's caress would spoil her hairdo. I prefer someone with a little more heart and fire, and less ice and vanity.'

'I picked you, Mr. Stuart,' Alisa chose her words carefully, 'because you come from a family of breeding. Despite your lack of a personal fortune, you're considered quite eligible by the people I associate with. You're not some pampered, mollycoddled fool who's incapable of making a decision on his own. You strike me as being a mercenary individual who would go to great lengths to get what he wanted. Right now, you want money.'

There was a long silence following Alisa's statement. When Zachary did reply, his voice was light and lightly amused.

'You don't hold a very high opinion of me, do you?'

'I don't hold a very high opinion of any man, Mr. Stuart,' Alisa answered contemptuously.

'And how do you feel about love?'

'The act or the emotion?' She accepted the cigarette he offered while glancing at him with frigid coldness.

'Not that it matters, since my opinion of them both is equally low. The first is disgusting and degrading and the second is a trap laid by men to ensure that women do their bidding.'

'Perhaps in the twelve months that you live with me, I might teach you a different understanding of love.' His dark eyes raked over her face and body with their obvious message. 'But,' with an expressive shrug of indifference, 'you'd probably be too difficult a pupil and take up too much of my time.'

'I'm glad you feel that way, because this is a business arrangement only!' Alisa emphasized harshly. 'I take it you're accepting my offer.'

'With a few conditions.'

'Which are?'

'First of all, the two hundred thousand is mine to do with as I please. Whether our marriage lasts a week or a year, it's mine as my price for allowing you to take my name.' Zachary smiled at the insolent curl of Alisa's lips for his condescending attitude. 'Secondly, while we're married, you will live where I live and off my own earnings. I assure you, my home is quite comfortable and my table well set. Finally, I'm sure your rigid pride will allow you to agree with me that no one outside of ourselves should know that this is a business arrangement for our own mutual benefit. Therefore I hope that in the company of our friends and family you will at least make an effort to display a fondness towards me.'

'Is that all?' She made no effort to hide the cutting sarcasm brought on by her growing anger. 'Has your male ego been satisfied?'

'For the time being. When is the marriage to take place?'

Alisa stared at the almost satanic pleasure in his expression, silently wishing that the freezing scorn in her own eyes would bring the usual discomfort that most men had shown under that gaze, but he was impervious to it.

'The sooner the better.' She gathered the black lace shawl around her shoulders and rose from her chair as he simultaneously joined her.

'I'll make the necessary arrangements,' Zachary announced, extending his hand to her.

With ill grace, Alisa placed her hand in his, wondering if this symbolic act of shaking hands to seal an agreement was really an act of putting her future in the hands of doom.

'How strange,' Zachary murmured, glancing down at their clasped hands. 'Your hand is cool.'

'So?' She attempted to withdraw it, but he held it firmly.

'Haven't you heard the saying, "Cold hands, warm heart"?' He was laughing at her again behind those fiery bright eyes.

'That's a silly old wives' tale.' Finally managing to free her hand, she turned away from him and began to walk towards the casino area.

'I'd be careful if I were you.' Zachary was at her side almost immediately, his large hand imprisoning her elbow. 'You already have one warm spot in your ice-encrusted heart for your sister. Some day a fire might come along and melt the rest away.'

'I'm completely immune to the type of fire you're

talking about.' She turned her frosty blue eyes towards his jeering smile.

'Which brings up another point. I'm not immune to the fires of passion, unlike you. Since this is quite obviously to be a marriage in name only, I sincerely hope that you don't expect me to embrace the vows of celibacy for an entire year.'

'Go ahead and have your disgusting little affairs,' Alisa said calmly, while allowing her distaste to show. 'Just have the decency, if you can, to keep them discreet. Now, if you'll excuse me, I see a friend waiting for me.'

'Certainly,' Zachary agreed smoothly. 'I'll call you at ten to inform you of the time and place of "our" wedding. What room are you in?'

Alisa gave him the information, disliking the imperious look on his face as if he were doing her a favour. As quickly as she could and with as much dignity and composure as she could, she left his side to join her cousin, who as usual, was completely engrossed at the dice tables.

When Alisa had finally dragged him away from the tables, and informed him of her coming marriage to Zachary Stuart, Michael had been shocked and outspokenly against it. He knew a great deal more about Zachary Stuart than he had told his cousin, mostly because he never dreamed that the man would even consider such a proposition as Alisa had put to him, let alone agree to it. His words of warning were wasted when he tried to explain to her that Stuart was a ruthless and merciless man when it came to getting what he wanted, that he could be extraordinarily cruel to those who had incurred his displeasure, and that he had no qualms about making advances towards his friends; women, unmarried or not, willing or not, though it was seldom that the women weren't willing.

But Alisa had turned a deaf ear to it all, confident that she could handle any situation. In her twenty-four years she had learned how to field the passes that were thrust upon her. Zachary Stuart might prove to be a more formidable opponent, she had declared, but he was still just a man, not some all-powerful demon as Michael was trying to make her believe. As a matter of fact, she had found him to be very amenable during their discussion. His occasional jibes and several references to crude subjects had been irritating and disgusting, but certainly nothing that couldn't be handled as long as she didn't let her irritation give way to anger and remained cool and composed. Besides, she was getting Christine, and that was the whole object.

No matter how deeply Alisa buried her head under the silk-encased pillow the persistent knocking wouldn't stop. Drowsily she realized that she had dozed off to sleep after her wake-up call. Bleary-eyed, she stared at her wristwatch on the bedside table – nine-forty-five! It must be Room Service, she decided, with her breakfast. Fighting the sleep that clung to her heavy lids, Alisa crawled out of bed, grabbing the robe that matched her pale blue nightgown from the chair before walking over to unlatch the door and hold it open.

She stared in blinking disbelief at the tall, dark man standing in her doorway. Self-consciously her hand

27

reached up to the lace ribbons that held the yoked neck of her robe together.

'Good morning.' Zachary moved easily past her into the room.

'You said you would call ... at ten.' She tried to inject a cold censure in her voice, but it ended up sounding like what it was, a surprised and embarrassed protest.

'I changed my mind and decided to stop instead,' he answered, seating himself in one of the plush blue velvet chairs before returning his attention to her to stare with uncomfortable thoroughness.

'Have you changed your mind about the wedding?' Alisa managed to ask calmly as if his answer didn't matter to her at all. With a great deal of control, she reached for her cigarette case on the bedside table, removed a cigarette, and lit it without any visible trembling such as was coursing through her.

'No.' His gaze drifted over the pale blue robe that curled around her ankles, its soft material clinging to her legs, hips, and waist before stopping at the high yoked neckline with petite capped sleeves. 'I wanted to see what my prospective bride looked like in the morning. I like the peignoir. It's like you, prudishly demure and provocatively sensuous.' She glared at him coldly before seating herself in the chair opposite him, taking great care to gather the robe around her tightly. 'It's a comfort to discover that Miss Perfect can look as dishevelled as any other normal woman in the morning.'

Alisa turned quickly to glance at her reflection in the gilt-edged mirror on the wall. A pale face stared back at her, scrubbed clean of make-up the night before. Her hair was all tousled, and there was a red welt on her cheek where she had lain on her arm.

'Damn! Why did he have to come when she was looking like this?' she thought angrily.

One corner of his mouth lifted in mocking amusement which only made Alisa angrier, although she took pains not to let it show.

'Why are you here, Stuart?'

'I'm your future husband. You should call me Zachary,' he replied with a cynical smile. 'I thought we'd get the marriage licence this morning. I've made arrangements for the ceremony to take place this afternoon at two, which gives us time to catch a flight out of Vegas any time after three.'

For a moment the speed with which he was arranging things surprised her, until Alisa realized his motive.

'You're awfully anxious to get your hands on the money, aren't you?' she snapped bitterly.

'You could change your mind.' His dark brows raised in challenge. Then, as if he was tired of playing the word game, he stubbed out his cigarette and rose from the chair. 'I'll meet you in the lobby in half an hour. From there we can get the licence, have lunch, and then go to the church.'

Alisa stiffened at the commanding tone of his voice. Right now she was in agreement that everything should be done as quickly as possible, but he might as well know now that she was equally capable of snapping out orders.

'Very well,' she said, 'you can book us on a flight to

San Francisco this afternoon. Tomorrow morning we'll go to the bank and I'll have a draft made out to you. Then we can stop in Oakland to pick up Christine.'

Zachary smiled lazily at her clipped words, seemingly amused by her attempt to exert authority over him, but he nodded agreement and repeated that he would meet her in the lobby in half an hour.

CHAPTER TWO

ALISA studied the thick black hair of the man behind the wheel and the dark brows that succeeded in making his eyes appear as fiery black coals. He was wearing a white polo shirt with a loden green sports jacket which accented the olive tan of his complexion. This was her husband.

Amid the fantasy world of Las Vegas with its myriad neon lights and dancing fountains, her actions had seemed quite reasonable and practical. The difference between winning and losing before had depended on the throw of the dice or the turn of the card, but now it had been ironically decided by her signature on a marriage certificate. She had won custody of Christine, but what had she lost?

Would she ever shake off the air of misgiving that had possessed her when the taxi had stopped outside the church the day before? The driver's snickering looks and sly innuendoes had sickened Alisa as Zachary had tipped him generously and sent him on. She had chided her trembling hands for their nervousness as she smoothed the white eyelet lace of her dress over its underlining of pale blue. The matching cloth hat had a tiny artificial bouquet of orange blossoms fastened on the wide floppy brim. Her pale gold hair was smoothly coiled in its austere chignon.

This was a silly, ritualistic ceremony, she had told herself, nothing to warrant this sudden attack of nerves. These vows they were going to take had no meaning. As a witness to three of her mother's weddings, she was an authority on that. Once inside the church, her poise had still been rattled. She had tried to jeer at the woman witness who had quickly shoved a handkerchief in Alisa's hand, whispering 'something borrowed'.

Zachary's voice had been calm and clear as he had made his vows. Whereas Alisa's had been low and tense, revealing her rigid control. That control had almost broken when she stumbled over the words, 'honour and *obey*' and glanced up into Zachary's mocking eyes. They had laughed at her twice more. Once when he slipped the plain gold band on her finger and again when she had perfunctorily brushed his lips with her own.

His goading had continued, whether directly or indirectly. Yesterday at the airport and later at the hotel when he had booked separate rooms, Zachary had been very specific in identifying her only as his wife, Mrs. Stuart. Even this morning at the bank, it had turned out that her banker was a close friend of his family and she had been once again pushed into the background. Her identity had been lost. Now she was just Zachary Stuart's wife. And he was taking pleasure in making sure she understood that fact. How she hated and despised him for it!

'Is this the house?' Zachary slowed the car down in front of an austere white two-storey house, the lawn immaculate, the shrubberies meticulously trimmed.

'Yes,' Alisa answered breathlessly, her blue eyes searching eagerly for the auburn head of her sister. But the closed doors and blank windows stared back unwelcomingly.

Alisa waited impatiently as Zachary manoeuvred the car into the driveway and walked around to open her door. Her sparkling eyes and quickened steps betrayed her excitement.

'You really do care about the child.' Zachary courteously took her arm as they reached the porch steps.

'Of course I do,' Alisa asserted, hurrying past the elegant yet severe white lawn furniture that looked as if it belonged in a Victorian garden.

In response to the chiming bells, the door was opened by an elderly woman, her iron-grey hair braided into a coronet on top of her head, her posture rigidly erect.

'Alisa!' Her false smile of welcome was mirrored by the irritation showing in her small dark eyes. 'I was so surprised when you called me this morning and said you were married.' The woman's gaze turned briefly on Zachary. 'This is your husband?' The sarcastic intonation wasn't lost on Alisa.

'Zachary Stuart,' Alisa introduced impatiently. 'My mother's sister-in-law, Marguerite Denton. Where is Christine?'

'You must come in and have some coffee.' The woman opened the door wider, completely ignoring Alisa's question as she led them through the darkly panelled hallway into an equally sombre room already set with a silver coffee service.

'You two were married in quite a hurry, weren't you?' Marguerite drawled. She seated herself immediately and began pouring the coffee.

'Once Alisa agreed, I didn't want to give her an opportunity to change her mind.' Zachary glanced down at his already seated wife with a show of fondness that bordered on mockery.

'Did you say you were only married yesterday?' Marguerite's malicious gaze flicked accusingly on Alisa as she handed her a fragile china cup. 'You two haven't even had a honeymoon. I'll be glad to take care of Christine if you want to go away for a few weeks.'

'That won't be necessary,' said Alisa.

'Not that we don't appreciate your offer,' Zachary inserted quickly, a very charming smile enhancing the softness of his words. 'We're more interested in making sure Christine understands that Alisa hasn't deserted her. We want her to know that she's a very important member of our family. You see how it is?'

'Yes, I do.' Marguerite's mouth trembled in ill-concealed anger, staring from one to the other.

'Where is Christine?' Alisa asked again.

'She was terribly overwrought this morning when I told her you were married.' A smug smile brought a bright gleam to the woman's eyes. 'She had settled down quite nicely here. It's unfortunate that she must be disrupted.'

'Where is she, Aunt Marguerite?'

'In her room. I made her lie down for a while.'

'Will you get her or shall I?' Alisa threatened. Her eyes sparkled with penetrating coldness.

'I'll get her.' The woman rose abruptly and left the room. The smoke of her anger was nearly visible.

As Marguerite left the room, Alisa reached nervously for a cigarette, chiding herself for allowing her aunt to rile her. Zachary quickly snapped open his lighter, offering the flame to the tip of the cigarette. Her gaze glittered on his face, irritated that he had stepped in to offer an explanation to her aunt for their speedy marriage. Marguerite hadn't been at all fooled.

Reading her thoughts, Zachary said, 'She may have her doubts as to the reason we're married, but there's no need for her to know for sure. It would only give her another weapon.'

'I can handle her,' Alisa asserted, exhaling slowly the smoke from her cigarette. 'She has no weapon.'

'Your fear of her and your love for Christine.'

Her eyes flashed quickly over Zachary, uncomfortably aware that he was entirely too discerning.

The sedate, even tread of Marguerite's footsteps in the hallway was accompanied by shuffling, reluctant, lighter steps. Alisa turned eagerly towards the doorway, her face brightening momentarily as a child appeared at her aunt's side. Although Alisa's arms opened, they remained empty as she stared at the sullenly lowered head of her sister.

'Chris?' she offered hesitantly, surprised at the complete lack of welcome.

The small brown head with its highlights of coppery red raised slightly, revealing a trembling chin and rebellious brown eyes. Christine's slender arms were tucked behind her back and the corners of her mouth were turned stubbornly down.

'I don't think Christine is very excited about seeing you.' A triumphant smile laughed out from Marguerite's face.

35

'That's not true!' Christine's head jerked up quickly, fixing her mutinous gaze on her aunt before turning to look at her sister. 'I'm supposed to tell you that I want to stay here, that I don't want to go with you.' Tears began brimming in the brown eyes. 'But I do, honest and truly I do!'

In the next instant, a small wiry body was flinging itself in Alisa's arms.

'Take her!' Marguerite called out shrilly, her malevolent eyes returning Alisa's accusing look. 'She's nothing but a nuisance anyway with her whining and insolence and running through the house. She's a spoiled brat. Just exactly what you'd expect of Eleanor's child!'

'Take Chris to the car, Alisa. I'll handle this.' The smouldering anger in Zachary's eyes nearly took her breath away when Alisa turned a grateful glance on him.

She clutched Christine to her tightly and hurried past her irate aunt, then down the hallway and out the door. Once in the car, Alisa disentangled the slender arms from around her neck, dried the twin trail of tears from her sister's cheeks, and reassured her that she didn't have anything to worry about any more. After the elfin face had finally managed to portray a hesitant smile, Alisa glanced towards the house. Her eyes gleamed with anticipation of what was going on in there. Even she had been intimidated by Zachary's authoritative voice and she wished she could have witnessed his confrontation with Marguerite.

Through most of her life, Alisa had dealt with things on her own. Her mother had always seemed to be too involved with a beau or husband when Alisa's childhood and teenage crises occurred. She had never known the security of a family unit. Dale Patterson had made her mother ecstatically happy and they had both attempted to draw Alisa into the circle of their love. But she had grown too cynical for her young years to accept their offer at the time. Alisa had been appalled when her mother had informed her that she was going to have a baby at the age of thirty-seven. Although Alisa had loved her new sister dearly, she was never quite a part of the new family, always standing back increasing her reserve unless she was alone with Christine. It was on her sister that she had poured out all the love that she couldn't safely give to anyone else.

The knowledge that Zachary was in that house doing battle with the aunt she despised was a new sensation to Alisa. The glow of gratitude was still on her face when Zachary came striding out of the house carrying a small suitcase in one hand. Not that she had needed him to fight for her, she reprimanded herself quickly. After all, she was quite capable of handling Marguerite herself. But, as much as she hated his mocking arrogance, Alisa knew she would never forget his show of kindness.

As he slid into the driver's seat, Alisa studied the stern lines of repressed anger still in his face. A shiver of fear scared away the softness she had felt earlier while she shuddered at the thought of what it would be like to be the recipient of his anger.

Sliding the key into the ignition, Zachary glanced at the pair, Alisa watching him with an outward calm and Christine peeping at him from the security of her sister's shoulder. His hands rested on the steering wheel as the banked fire of his gaze swept over them.

'I picked up a few things for Christine. The rest will be sent on to our home.'

Alisa's jaw tightened at the possessive coupling of her and Christine to him. The corners of his mouth twisted upward at her noticeable stiffening.

A trace of animosity beamed through Christine's brown eyes as she studied Zachary. 'She said you didn't like little girls.' Although her chin trembled, Christine spoke quite forcefully. 'She said you wouldn't want me around and that you'd be packing me back if I did anything bad.'

Zachary's eyes flared briefly at Alisa.

'Christine is referring to Marguerite,' Alisa smiled, coolly dismissing his accusing look with a hint of contempt.

'Your aunt was wrong, Chris.' He met Alisa's disdainful stare with an amused smile. 'I like little girls very much, especially when they grow up to be big girls as pretty as your sister. And I'm sure your sister will do everything she can, regardless of what you do or how bad you are, to make sure you never go back to your aunt.' With mocking arrogance, his eyes travelled over Alisa, taking in the creamy perfection of her face and neck and the becoming way her beige plaid jacket clung to her curves. As if satisfied with what he saw, Zachary turned away, started the car, and began backing it out of the driveway.

'She said you would want Lisa all to yourself, that you wouldn't want me hanging around her,' Christine persisted, needing all her fears to be smoothed away.

'I'll tell you what we'll do.' His eyes never left the street ahead of them as he replied in a gentle, though amused voice. 'I work during the day so you can have Alisa all to yourself then. At night-time when you have to go to bed, then Alisa will be with me. How's that?'

'Fine.' But there was a hesitancy in the child's voice that brought Zachary's gaze around to glance at her curiously. At the compelling question in his eyes, Christine added, 'My daddy had to work, too, but sometimes he did things with Mommy and me. We had a lot of fun.' The fervent unasked question brought a slow spreading smile to his face.

'I think the three of us could have a lot of fun, too. Don't you, Alisa?'

A cold, burning anger was welling up inside Alisa. The newly implanted seed of softness towards the dark-haired man who was her husband had rapidly succumbed to the killing frost. She could see through his ruse of reassuring words to her baby sister and read the laughing assertion that despite any claims by her to the contrary, she was dependent on him, that she needed him for the sake of the child. He should feel subjugated to her. That was the way she had planned it, that he would be under obligation to her.

'Won't it be fun, Lisa?' Christine's plaintive voice broke into her musing.

Alisa glanced down at the earnest little face, forcing a smile that she was far from feeling.

'Zachary will be very busy, so we can't expect him to spend very much time with us. In fact, very little at all, but when he does, I'm sure it will be quite enjoyable for you.'

39

The jeering chuckle was like the scrape of chalk against a blackboard. 'This is only the summer, my dear. Harvest season, the busy time, begins in August. There'll be plenty of time for all of us to do things together before then.' Zachary flashed his mocking smile at her.

Christine clapped her hands together in delight, her happiness too important to Alisa for her to dampen it so soon.

'Where are we going now?' Christine asked. Her brown eyes, still lit with the lamp of joy, gazed out the car window at the whirl of traffic around them.

'To our home in Napa Valley,' Zachary told her.

'Where's that?' she persisted.

'About an hour and a half's drive from San Francisco.' He smiled gently at the soft brown, inquiring eyes.

Satisfied, Christine settled down in the seat between Alisa and Zachary, contentment etched on her face, in the pertness of her nose and the elfin glow on her face.

The car turned off the Silverado Trail between two winged brick pillars connected by a wrought iron arch enscrolled with the name Stuart Vineyards. A cordon of massive oak trees hovered protectively over the narrow lane. Their trunks and limbs were gnarled and weathered by the years they had stood as sentinels over the gravelled road. Gaping holes studded with grave-like stumps marked the places where age had thinned their ranks. Beyond the thick foliage of their branches lay the vineyards where the dark green leaves of the vines were like the waves of the sea rolling over the sloping hills.

Alisa shielded her eyes from the heavy midday sun when Zachary slowed the car down, approaching a awning split in the lane. The corridor of trees fell away to reveal a circular drive. Nestled on the far side of the circle amidst more stands of giant oak trees was a two-and-a-half-storey brick home, its turrets and cupolas and gables daring an ordinary roof to compete with its uniqueness. Around the arched, white-trimmed windows and doors clung tenacious Boston ivy, its green leaves hiding the dark red brick exterior. Another narrow lane branched off the circular drive and led towards the rear of the house before breaking away to go up the hill behind it to another set of buildings. Alisa was stunned by the magnificence of the estate. She had fully expected to be taken to a modest winery with one of those common little houses that always seemed dwarfed by the winery buildings themselves. The lawns were immaculate. There was a small flower garden on the south side of the house. A small patio was on the same side, with plushly cushioned white rattan lawn furniture.

Christine was chattering at Zachary, who had stopped the car and was already opening the door on Alisa's side. His dark eyes mocked her quickly moving gaze as she tried to take in the old-world elegance of his home. A horrible nagging thought struck her. This didn't look like the home of a poor man!

'The plumbing is a bit temperamental, but I think you'll find everything else to your satisfaction, Mrs. Stuart,' Zachary said solemnly while taking her hand as she stepped out of the car.

'It's very impressive.' Although she attempted to pu[t] an air of nonchalance in her voice, it mixed rathe[r] falsely with genuine wonder. 'Hardly what I was led t[o] believe.'

'But then you never asked me to substantiate any [of] your information.' Apprehension crept into her eyes [as] he forced her to meet his compelling look. 'What [I] needed money for was the expansion of my winery.'

Alisa breathed a silent sigh of relief. For a mome[nt] there, she had thought he was going to drop som[e] bombshell of information on her. She glanced aroun[d] for Christine, who was already racing towards the ste[ps] of the house, calling them to hurry so that she coul[d] explore her new home. With a sardonically amuse[d] smile, Zachary took Alisa's arm and led her to the b[ig] white door with its large brass knocker where Christin[e] stood impatiently hopping from one foot to th[e] other.

'I want to see you carry Alisa through the door!' sh[e] cried, a wide smile beaming expectantly to each as the[y] reached her side.

'That's a silly superstition,' Alisa admonished, 'an[d] you know I don't believe in that kind of thing, Chri[s]tine.'

'Well, your husband does,' Zachary laughed, swee[p]ing her up easily in his arms and nodding to Chris t[o] open the door.

'Put me down!' Alisa whispered sharply, her fis[t] pushing stiffly at his broad chest.

'Why don't you relax and enjoy it?' A lazy twiste[d] smile laughed at her meagre protests.

'I don't see any enjoyment in a mans' arms,' Alisa answered. Her voice was still lowered, yet implicitly expressing her distaste of his touch.

'I could teach you a lot,' he murmured, one eyebrow arching to disappear in his dark hair while he crushed her tighter against him.

Giggling, Christine called from inside the door, 'Aren't you going to come in?'

Ignoring the rigidity with which Alisa tried to hold herself away from him, Zachary carried her over the threshold and into the foyer of the house. Once inside, he stopped, but still didn't put her down, smiling with amusement at the cold contempt in her face. At the sound of footsteps approaching from another room, he turned, letting her down only when a woman came into view. As the woman drew nearer, Christine hurried to Alisa, taking her hand for comfort. Zachary's arm was still around her waist, and with the approach of the woman, Alisa knew she must suffer it for a few minutes longer.

'Zach!' The grey-haired woman reached out to clasp his hand with both of hers, her pale blue eyes beaming up at him in happiness before she glanced curiously at Alisa and Christine. 'We didn't expect you back for another two days.'

'You know I couldn't stay away from my second best girl for a whole week,' Zachary teased, touching his lips to her cheek in an affectionate kiss.

At his use of the term 'second best', the woman looked again at Alisa. Her eyes anxiously surveyed the coolness in Alisa's gaze as well as the pale gold coiffure and the perfection of her beauty.

43

'Nora, I want you to meet my wife, Mrs Alisa Franklin Stuart.' There was the barest trace of mockery in his eyes as he gently nudged Alisa closer. 'And her sister Christine Patterson. Alisa, Chris, this is my housekeeper, Nora Castillo.'

Both Alisa and Nora glanced at Zachary in surprise. Alisa because she had never known a servant to be greeted with such welcome and affection. It was something that had never been done, not even by her romantic-minded mother. And Nora because of Zachary's announcement of his marriage. Alisa didn't care for the way the housekeeper studied her now that she knew Alisa was Mrs. Zachary Stuart. She had the peculiar feeling that she was a pound of meat in a butcher's shop that had been weighed and come up short. The woman was very evidently unaware of her place. Their mutual exchange of greetings was cool each in their own silent way showing the other their disapproval.

'Just a light lunch will do us, Nora.' Zachary broke into the hostile silence. 'We'll take it on the patio in about an hour. In the meantime, I'm going to check in with George. I'm sure Alisa would like to freshen up and Christine needs it.' He ruffled the brown head on the other side of Alisa briskly. 'Take Mrs. Stuart up to the Lavender Room.'

'The Lavender Room?' Nora repeated, a sharp glance cast accusingly at Alisa.

'Yes.' His tone definitely dismissed any further questioning. 'Is there anything you need from the car?'

Alisa shook her head negatively. 'I'll bring the cases up later, then,' Zachary finished.

44

His hand as it left the encirclement of her waist came up to brush her cheek in a feathery caress before he walked away. It had been all Alisa could do not to flinch away from his touch. His mocking glance had told her he knew it and so did the sharp eyes of the housekeeper.

'Where am I going to stay?' Christine pulled impatiently on Alisa's hand.

'Is there a room near mine?' asked Alisa, staring aloofly at the disapproving eyes of the grey-haired woman.

'Yes, down the hall is the Green Room. If you will follow me?' The heels of the housekeeper's shoes clicked across the marble tiled floor of the foyer as she led them towards the ornately carved open staircase.

The pale yellow walls blended smoothly with the oak woodwork and the traces of gold in the marbled floor. The steps of the staircase were overlaid with matching marble tiles, their width adding to the aura of wealth and elegance. At the top of the stairs, there was a rich carpet of gold to silence the sound of their feet. The wide hallway with its high ceiling and pale walls consisted of two branches from the stair landing, one leading to the left and the other to the right. Nora Castillo led Alisa and Christine to the right, where she paused at the first door on the left side.

'This is the room we call the Green Room,' she announced, opening the door and stepping inside.

Alisa walked on past the housekeeper into the room, with Christine following shyly behind her. The walls were a cool spring green with the woodwork painted white to match the gilded white French Provincial bedroom set. The single bed had a gay canopy with a myriad of floral bouquets printed on the white chintz cloth, which matched the bedspread and curtains.

'It's like a bed for a princess!' Christine stared at the canopy, her eyes filled with the magic of the thought. She turned to Alisa. 'Is it really my room?'

Alisa nodded, her face glowing with the happiness reflected in her little sister's eyes.

'The bath is through this door,' Nora stated as she opened a white-enamelled door, 'with a connecting door to your room, Mrs. Stuart.'

Instantly at the sound of the housekeeper's voice, the smile on Alisa's face faded. The icy aloofness returned as she ordered Mrs. Castillo to show her her room. Again Alisa was met by superb decorating taste as she stepped into the Lavender Room behind the housekeeper. As before there were pale walls and white woodwork, except the accent was elegance as echoed by the Italian Provincial furniture and the deep purple velvet bedspread and curtains with an inset of the palest lavender sheets. Underfoot was a plush ivory carpet.

'The master bedroom where Zach sleeps is in the next room.' Nora Castillo clearly stated her displeasure in the separate bedroom arrangement.

'Is there a connecting door?' Alisa asked quickly, glancing at the wall that separated them.

'No.' The pale blue eyes of the housekeeper blinked challengingly at Alisa. 'Would you care to see the master bedroom?'

'No, I do not. I don't believe I'll need you for anything else.' Alisa dismissed her sharply, not liking the

46

woman's familiar attitude.

For a moment Alisa stared at the door that had closed behind the retreating woman before Christine came bursting through the connecting bathroom door.

'Isn't it wonderful? Your room is pretty like mine, too. Oh, can I go exploring I've washed my hands and got cleaned up.'

Alisa smiled broadly and hugged the dancing girl to her. The warmth of her love for her sister brought a faint misting of tears to Alisa's eyes as she released her. She shooed Christine out of the room, reminding her of lunch in a little less than an hour and for her not to stray out of the garden. When silence once more permeated the room, Alisa sank into the velvet-cushioned chair in front of the dressing-table, her fingers reaching up to rub her temples.

The woman looking back at her from the mirror looked strangely alien with her smooth skin, pale gold hair, and her clear, untroubled eyes. No matter how many times Alisa looked in the mirror and no matter how pleased she was with the attractive girl who stared back, she was always a bit surprised by what she saw. She wanted to see someone as free and as happy as Christine, as full of life and love, but always the same cool eyes stared back at her, reminding her that she was much too vulnerable and that she had gone through a great deal of pain to acquire this total composure.

Life was not the wildly happy thing that the fairy tales had once led her to believe. She was better off knowing the truth of the reality and not wrapped up in rose-coloured spectacles, she told herself. All those romantic stories were a farce designed to lead one on in false hope. The love of a child, of Christine, was the only safe thing she could cling to, the only thing she could trust.

Alisa rose abruptly, removed the beige plaid jacket, tossed it on the bed, and hugged her arms about the beige shell as she walked to the window. She knew what kind of a woman the housekeeper was, one that believed in the age-old place of a woman in marriage, the traditional wife subservient to her husband, willing to be mistress, mother, and maid to him.

'Isn't the room to your taste?' Zachary stood inside the doorway, her suitcase at his feet.

'It's a very lovely room. Who wouldn't be satisfied with it?' Alisa answered indifferently. The startled light at his unexpected appearance now gone from her eyes.

'You.' His dark eyes studied her thoroughly from the tips of her sporty ivory heels to the top of her ivory blonde hair. 'I should have thought by this time that you would have found something about my home you don't like.'

'I'll only be living here one year,' rising to his sarcasm. 'It would hardly be worthwhile to do any redecorating for that short time.'

'And Nora? What do you think of her?'

'I think she's much too familiar for a servant, regardless of how good she might be.' Alisa met his intense, questioning gaze, bolstered by her own bitterness at any supposed depth of feeling between two adults.

'What would you suggest? That I get rid of her ...

48

for the duration?' Zachary seemed to bristle in anger, although his voice was calm, almost amused.

'I think it's an excellent suggestion,' Alisa returned, 'but rather a drastic one. The best thing to do is to have a talk with her and make sure she knows that she's a servant.'

'You're a snob as well as a bitch! There'll be no talk with Nora.' His eyes gleamed with a satanic fire while the breadth of his chest dwarfed her as he stepped closer. 'If anyone goes, it will be you, Mrs. Stuart.' Zachary laughed shortly with amusement and contempt at the frustration in her face. 'But then you can't leave, can you? and still keep Christine.'

'I think you're an insufferable, dominating boor, Mr. Stuart!' Alisa refused to display the anger that was raging inside. To do so would be a show of weakness that she couldn't allow to happen. Instead she spoke with a steady, analytical voice. 'I think I've made you feel insecure. Although you demanded a high price to marry me, the fact that I was able to pay galls you. Now you feel you must reassert your ego by obtaining the upper hand with me through blackmail. You won't succeed, my dear husband,' with cool sarcasm, 'because I have what I want and you can't make me give up.'

Her head turned so her eyes could meet his gaze, their haughty coolness emphasizing the conviction of her voice. But Zachary was unmoved by it. He studied her with mocking interest as he slowly brought the flame of his lighter closer to the cigarette in his mouth.

'You're right – I am interested in making you give up.' Through the thin veil of exhaled smoke, Alisa could see him laughing at her, jeering at her words. 'But I don't think we're talking about the same thing.'

'Well, I don't propose to have any cryptic conversation with you,' she retorted sharply. 'You did say lunch was to be ready in an hour. Let's go down now.'

'Is that an invitation or an order?' Zachary asked as Alisa walked past him to the door. She stopped at the door, her head turning slightly back towards him at the almost ominous softness of his voice.

'Whichever you please.'

'I don't take orders, especially from my wife.' A slow lazy smile played about the hard lines of his mouth as she turned sharply at his reply.

'How quaint!' Her voice was deliberately edged with sarcasm. 'Perhaps you could learn.'

'If there's any learning to be done, it will be by you and I will be the teacher.' His gaze locked challengingly with hers.

Alisa read the powerful intimidation in his eyes, the dare to continue trying to dispute him. Unwillingly she remembered Michael's statement that Zachary Stuart could be ruthless and unrelenting. But then he'd never met anyone like her before.

'Frankly, you couldn't teach me anything. And furthermore, I don't care if you have lunch with me or not. I have no desire to sit at a table with you. As far as I'm concerned you can crawl back under the woodwork where you came from!' With complete poise, Alisa stepped out of the room into the hallway.

'You really would like me to vanish into thin

50

air.' His mocking voice told her Zachary was only a step behind her as she walked to the stair landing. 'You can't walk through me as if I weren't here. And I'll never allow you to walk over me.'

'Then, Mr. Stuart,' she smiled back at him with brittle sweetness, 'I will walk around you.'

His left eyebrows lifted in amused disbelief while his calloused hand gripped her elbow as they started down the marble inlaid stairs. 'If you can,' he replied.

Christine's slight shyness of her strange new home had disappeared by lunch. And it was her chattering that had covered the frosty silence of her older sister. Zachary had been indulgent with Christine, but totally indifferent to Alisa. He had seemed to expect her silence with an attitude that said 'go ahead and isolate yourself, it doesn't hurt me in the slightest'. That had angered Alisa. By the time the dessert of fresh fruit had been eaten, she was seething with rage at his lack of interest. She had expected that he wouldn't attempt to coax her into the conversation, but she had thought he would at least make some pointed remark about her continuing silence. He hadn't. Zachary had excused himself from the table to Christine, saying that he had work to do at the vineyard office on the hill.

The black German police dog who had been waiting patiently at the edge of the patio had padded over to Zachary's side and followed him as Zachary had made his way through the trees towards the building further up the hill from the house. Alisa suffered Christine's exclamations about the dog, named Baron, with whom Christine had made friends before lunch. At last Alisa broke through the outpourings of her sister to announce that they would unpack their clothes and then tour the house and grounds the rest of the afternoon.

Since most of their clothes had not arrived yet, it took very little time to unpack and put away their things. Christine immediately insisted on being Alisa's guide, taking her by the hand as they stepped out of Alisa's bedroom into the hall and motioning that the rooms on the opposite end of the hall were only bedrooms for guests. Chris skipped down the stairs ahead of her sister, opened the double doors on the left, and in her most authoritative voice announced that this was the formal living-room. Alisa had a brief moment to admire the comfortable traditional furniture in the airy room of creamy white softness before she was whisked into the dining-room. Again, allowed only the shortest pause, Alisa could see that the large yet intimate room would easily transform itself from the needs of a small group to a very large one with no difficulty. Another set of double doors were opened.

'This is my favourite room!' Christine danced around a plush yellow flowered sofa that matched the bright yellow walls with its white-trimmed woodwork. In front of the large latticed windows sat a small drop-leaf table of snowy white. A large recliner chair of dull gold was in the corner. 'Nora said this is the morning-room. Do you know why it's named that?' Chris asked. At the negative shake of her sister's head, Christine began to explain, 'Because this is where we have breakfast. She said nobody likes to go into the dining-room because it's so elegant, and nobody feels elegant in the morning!'

Alisa couldn't help agreeing. It was the perfect room to enter in the morning, bright and spacious to wake you up, yet filled with cosy, snuggly furniture where people who hadn't shaken the sleep from them could relax.

'The kitchen's through that door,' Chris went on, continuing her hectic pace back into the hall. 'But Nora said the cook doesn't like people messing about in her kitchen.'

The pair had arrived back to the entrance foyer where Chris paused in front of a set of double doors opposite the living-room.

'This is the "lion's room",' she giggled.

'The "lion's room"?' Alisa repeated.

'That's what Mommy and I used to call it.' A slightly wistful expression appeared in her brown eyes. 'Daddy called it his den at home, but he used to roar so if anyone disturbed him that we called it the "lion's room". Nora said that this was Zachary's room where he works sometimes and that I wasn't supposed to go in there.'

'Yes, Zachary would very likely roar at you, too.' Alisa compressed her lips in a firm line, although her voice carried a light note. 'But you shouldn't call the housekeeper Nora. Her name is Mrs. Castillo.'

'I told her to call me Chris and she said I could call her Nora,' the little girl shrugged. 'Besides, that's what Zach calls her, so it's all right.'

'That's true, he does call her Nora. But it's proper for a young girl to call her elders by their surname. It shows respect,' Alisa insisted, irritated by Chris's sudden reference to Zachary as if he were the authority.

53

'But then I'd have to call you Mrs. Stuart.' The brown eyes widened with innocence.

'I'm your sister, so it's different. I'm a member of your family.'

'So's Nora. She said so and Zach did, too.' The auburn hair seemed to glow with a slightly redder hue as Christine's stubbornness began to set in.

'We'll discuss it later,' knowing that until she had an opportunity to talk to Zachary and straighten him out, it was useless to argue with Christine. 'I think we should go upstairs and change into some shorts before we explore outside.'

The auburn hair bounced wildly as Christine's slender young body tried to keep up with her ever-whirling skipping rope. The late afternoon sun cast a grotesque shadow of the girl, distorted, making her all legs and arms as she counted the number of times her sandalled feet hopped over the spinning rope until at last it tangled in her feet and she collapsed in the chair beside Alisa.

'How many was that?' she asked, gasping for breath from her exertions.

'Sixty-two,' Alisa replied. Her blue eyes smiled brightly at her red-faced sister.

'It was not! It was forty-nine times,' she corrected crossly.

'How do you know?' Alisa teased.

'Because I counted.'

'If you were counting, then why did you ask me to count?'

'If I make you count for me, I know you'll watch

me,' Christine grinned impishly.

'You silly goose, I always watch you.' The aloofness that usually marred the perfect features had been erased by the laughter and love for the child seated in front of Alisa.

Christine stirred restlessly. 'Let's go up to those buildings on the hill and find out what Zach's doing.'

'I told you we weren't going up there.' There was a slightly vicious movement as Alisa snubbed out her cigarette. That had been a repeated request that she had denied practically the entire afternoon. The last thing she wanted to do was show an interest in what he was doing.

'Supper's at seven o'clock. Don't you think we should tell him?'

'You mean dinner,' Alisa corrected.

'Dinner – supper, it's almost time to eat.' A mutinous scowl clouded the girl's face at her sister's evasion.

'I'm sure he's aware of what time we eat without being told.'

'I'm going up there whether you do or not,' Christine rose, drawing as much adult indignation into her words and manner as she could.

'Christine, don't be difficult.'

'I'm not being difficult. You're being difficult!' The lashes of her brown eyes fluttered widely as Christine lifted her shoulder in a defiant gesture.

'You're being rude!' Alisa retorted sharply. 'I told you not to go up there. If you're so interested in seeing Zachary then you can walk up to that big tree and wait for him. But you are not going to the winery, and that's final!'

Christine's temper flared brightly as she stalked off towards the distant tree while Alisa sighed in exasperation. Her sister had been so spoiled by her mother that she resented not getting her own way. Alisa had been just as guilty before, allowed by her love for the child with the pixie haircut and pointed chin to be wheedled and coaxed into anything that would bring that happy smile to Christine's face. It was just as well that Chris learned now that she couldn't have everything her own way.

Uncrossing her legs, Alisa slowly rose to her feet, her hand reaching up to adjust the puffed sleeve of her light green blouse and smooth the wide ruffles of the scooped neck. From a near chair, she gathered her long hostess skirt and fastened it around her waist over her shorts, then buttoned it half-way down the front, leaving the rest open so that the light golden colour of her legs would be set off by the white linen skirt. She had rearranged her hair earlier in the afternoon into an old-fashioned Gibson girl style that lent a delicate air to her face.

The crunching of tyres upon the gravelled drive drew her attention. The car braked to a halt short of the front entrance and the driver stepped out of the car to stand by his door staring at Alisa on the patio. Slowly, as if his feet refused to obey, the man walked towards her.

'Alisa?' his questioning voice called, speaking her name with almost reverent stillness.

The stunned face below silky blond-brown hair grew clearer as he walked towards her. Long slender fingers reached out to capture her hands while earnest blue eyes searched her face and hair. Numbed by the realization that it was Paul Andrews whom she had dismissed so scathingly to Zachary, Alisa didn't even attempt to withdraw her hands from him.

'I thought you were a ghost. I couldn't believe my eyes when I saw you standing here when I drove in.' His voice was hardly more than a hoarse whisper as he gazed at her in undisguised adoration. 'What are you doing here?' As Alisa opened her mouth to explain, he shook his head to silence her. 'You don't have to tell me. I've already guessed. Zachary brought you, didn't he?' She nodded 'yes' and tried again to speak, but he began to laugh with relieved pleasure. 'I've never had a friend like him before. Alisa – you wouldn't believe all he's done for me. When you told me you didn't want to ever see me again, I went to pieces. I hated the whole world! But Zach was there to put me together again. He must have guessed, though, that I still love you. That's it, isn't it? He brought you here so you could be with me.'

'Paul, stop!' Alisa protested. She felt pity and embarrassment growing inside her for this attractive but misguided man, where once he had only aroused disgust and indifference.

'I can't. I'm so deliriously happy!' When he tried to draw her into an embrace, Alisa pushed away.

'You don't understand!' she cried. 'It's not the way you're thinking!'

'What do you mean?' The almost pained look on Alisa's face brought Paul to a stop. His brow knitted into a frown as he suddenly noticed her unease.

'I didn't know you were going to be here,' she explained, regaining her poise and calming her voice.

'Zach meant to surprise us both, the old devil!' Paul laughed, then stopped short to stare at her again. 'You're more beautiful than I remembered.'

'Paul, I don't think Zachary is as much of a friend as you think he is,' Alisa tried to explain, and at the same time stay the hands that were trying to draw her nearer.

'That's a fine way for my wife to carry on the first time I turn my back!' Both Paul and Alisa whirled sharply at Zachary's laughingly contemptuous words. The dark eyes glowed with triumphant amusement as they captured Alisa's glance.

Paul had moved hastily away from Alisa and was now staring from her to Zachary in numbed disbelief. Without even a glance towards Paul, Zachary walked over and put an arm around Alisa's shoulders and crushed her to his side. He ignored her rigidness as he stared down into her frosty eyes with mock affection.

'She's everything you said she was, Paul, and a lot more.' Alisa knew Paul was too stricken to hear the sarcasm in Zachary's honeyed voice. 'I was going to phone you to tell you the good news. We were married yesterday in Las Vegas.'

The tanned face grew ghostly pale as Paul swallowed and managed a mumbled 'Congratulations'. But Zachary ignored the lack of enthusiasm and continued to allow his gaze to rest on Alisa's accusing face.

'I have to thank you, Paul, for allowing me so much insight on Alisa before I met her. Talk about a whirlwind courtship! I never gave her an opportunity to think about what she was doing until I was safely escorting her out of the church.'

'Marry in haste, repent in leisure,' Alisa drawled, and was rewarded for her spiteful teasing by the slowly gripping pressure of Zachary's hand around her arm until she bit her lips to keep from crying out her pain.

'That's not the kind of comment a new bride is supposed to make, my darling,' Zachary reprimanded. He would have kissed her, but Alisa turned her head so that his lips found her cheek instead. His eyes flashed their fires briefly on her before he released her and pushed her with mocking affection towards the house. 'Go, woman, and get us some sherry. It's time our wedding was toasted by someone other than ourselves.'

Alisa glanced hesitantly back at Paul and was sickened by the blank look that was etched on the gently strong features. She could understand how he would have attempted suicide when he felt he had lost her. The bitterness and pain was visible in the depths of his sea blue eyes. She knew the slight pity she felt was wasted, thanks to her husband. What irritated her as she walked towards the house was the callously cruel way that Zachary was dangling their marriage in front of Paul. Stabbing the man in the back would have been a less painless way to hurt him. Stepping through the French doors into the dining-room, Alisa knew that this sadistic display was in keeping with Zachary's behaviour.

When she returned with the small silver tray holding three crystal wine glasses and a decanter of dry sherry, Alisa found Zachary and Paul seated at the umbrellaed table. A bit of colour had returned to Paul's cheeks, although the haunted look was still in his blue eyes when he looked at her. After the wine had been poured and the glasses raised, Paul made a poignantly sincere wish for their happiness.

'Does Renée know yet?' Paul asked just as Zachary poured himself more sherry.

'No.' Zachary studied the tawny brown liquid in his glass before meeting the arched eyebrow of Alisa. Paul glanced nervously at her as if fearing he had committed a very bad faux pas.

'I really think you should phone her to let her know,' Paul suggested.

'Let her find out on her own. Or better yet, you tell her.' The dark eyes roved over Alisa's face and neck.

'Renée is one of Zachary's former girl-friends?' Alisa directed her cool voice to Paul.

'You have no reason to be jealous, my loving wife.' The slow, lazy smile spread wide to reveal the laughter in his expression. 'She's dark and petite and quite passionate. Not at all like the Snow Queen I married.'

'I'm sorry. I didn't mean to start an argument,' Paul apologized.

'Don't bother,' Zachary laughed, reaching out from his chair at the table to grasp Alisa's hand and pull her over to where she stood alongside him. His hand released her long enough for his arm to encircle her waist and to hold her there despite her attempts to wriggle away. 'I enjoy teasing my wife about her reluctance to show her love for me. But I'll soon cure her of that.'

'Stop it!' Alisa hissed as his free hand moved to rest his spread fingers on her stomach. When her own hand would have taken his and flung it away from her, he captured it instead, drawing it, despite her struggles, to his lips where he kissed the palm. His eyes danced their amusement at her frigid expression, not releasing her hand even when the caress was finished, knowing the curled fingers of her hand were longing to leave their imprint on his face.

'I have an idea. Why don't you stay to dinner, Paul?' Zachary asked. It sounded like an impulsive invitation, but Alisa felt sure that it had been carefully thought out.

'I couldn't. It's your first night here. Two's company, three's a crowd,' Paul reminded them bitterly.

'We already have a seven-year-old chaperone.' Zachary nodded towards Christine, who was busy throwing sticks for the dog to chase out on the lawn. 'One more and we'll have a party. We want you to stay, don't we, Alisa?'

'Maybe Paul has other plans,' she prompted.

'Then as his employer I order him to cancel them.' Zachary's eyes glittered at her with threatening fierceness before he turned a more amicable glance to Paul.

'Well, I . . .' Paul ran a hand through his blond hair while attempting to meet the intimidating sureness of Zachary's gaze.

'It's settled, then. Go tell Nora there'll be four for dinner,' Zachary ordered Alisa. The corners of his mouth turned up into a grim smile that challenged her to refuse.

Whether it was because of his arrogant certainty

61

that she would attempt to defy him, or because she herself had been intimidated by his air of dominance, Alisa calmly smiled her acquiescence to his command. With a politely murmured request to withdraw, she excused herself to enter the house.

Having informed the houskeeper that Mr. Stuart had invited Paul Andrews to join them for dinner that evening, Alisa remained in the house, mentally refusing to go out on the patio and be baited any further by Zachary. A quarter of an hour later Zachary entered the living-room where Alisa was idly flipping through a fashion magazine.

'So this is where you went to,' he remarked before explaining that Paul and Christine had gone to wash. 'Wasn't it rather rude not to rejoin us?'

'Not any more rude and insensitive than you've been,' she retorted, flipping the magazine shut and tossing it on the table in front of the blue sofa. 'How could you be so unfeeling as to invite him to dinner?'

With panther-like ease, Zachary lowered his tall frame into the matching chair, his head leaning against the back so that his bland stare could watch her.

'It's time he stopped thinking of you as some virginal goddess on a pedestal. The shock of discovering you're married to me will do him a world of good. By staying to dinner, he will acclimatize himself to the fact and face it before he goes off on his own to brood himself into some depressed and bitter mood.' He paused to study her with a sneering expression on his face. 'The dinner will also give you a chance to show me just how well you intend to accept the conditions of our marriage.'

'What are you talking about?' Alisa gazed at him contemptuously, her neck stiffening at his dictorial attitude.

'We agreed that in the company of others we would express a fondness for each other. And if that's what you've been attempting to do so far this evening, then, my love, you're a terrible actress.'

'If you think I'm going to allow you to caress me or embrace me every time someone comes into this house, you have another think coming!' Alisa exclaimed, rising to her feet in anger.

'You're exciting to look at, Alisa, but you're cold to the touch. An arm around your shoulder is hardly an embrace, and I have yet to caress you. I doubt very much if you have the experience to tell the difference.' He nonchalantly snapped his lighter to a cigarette, exhaling the smoke to cloud between them. 'I would be satisfied with a smile from you even though I know it would do severe damage to that mask you wear.'

'I can smile quite often, thank you,' she retorted sarcastically. 'And if a smile will keep you from embracing me, I'll smile all the time. I may not speak from experience, but I do speak from knowledge, and that was still an embrace.'

'Where did you gain all this great knowledge?' Zachary mocked.

'From a man.' Alisa's head tilted backwards in indignation.

'I doubt if you've ever known one.'

'My cousin Michael has been my constant companion for nearly five years.'

'That lapdog that followed you around in Vegas picking up any change you left behind!' Zachary rose to his feet, his jeering chuckle leaving no doubt his opinion of Michael. 'I repeat, you've never known a man.'

'I suppose you think you are.' Her eyes were haughty with scorn as she looked up at him when he stopped in front of her.

'Some day I may decide to prove it to you.' He seemed almost bored as he scanned her face and pale blonde hair.

'Don't waste your time!'

'I never do,' Zachary replied, shrugging his shoulders with emphasis. Glancing over her shoulder, he waved his hand. 'Here we are, Paul. Have you seen Christine?'

'She was skipping down the hall towards the dining-room as I was coming down the stairs,' Paul replied.

'I guess we're all ready to go in, then.' Zachary moved around so that Alisa was on one side and Paul on the other as he ushered them into the dining-room.

Christine was leaning against one of the chairs, one foot resting on the other while she glumly surveyed the elegant table setting with its candelabra and flowery centrepiece. The white bone china glistened, surrounded by polished silver and an array of sparkling crystal glasses as Christine turned her gloomy expression on them as they stepped to the table.

'What's the matter?' Alisa asked in a low voice as she held the chair for her sulky half-sister before pushing it up to the table.

'I bet I never get to have hamburgers and french fries here!' Christine made no attempt to lower her voice and it rang out with embarrassing clarity.

Zachary's laughter drowned out Alisa's attempt to reprimand Chris. 'Don't scold her. She's just being honest,' he told Alisa. 'I think we can arrange something with the cook so that you can have your hamburgers and french fries occasionally. How's that, Chris?'

'Fine!' Her brown eyes glowed to match the shimmering highlights of her auburn hair.

'But this is the first dinner that you and Alisa have had in your new home and I think Mrs. March wanted to impress you both,' Zachary explained, astounding Alisa with his patience and ability to appeal for Christine's understanding.

There was no gentleness in his face. There was no room for gentleness in the hard features. Alisa decided it was the authority in his tone that had reached Christine – and again she experienced the growing irritation at his ability to dominate all who came in contact with Zachary Stuart. All except herself; she would remain unmoved by him. He could command anyone else that he wished, be the lord of the manor to whoever was willing to kneel at his feet, but never would she acknowledge him.

Alisa immediately took charge of the conversation, centring her attention on Paul Andrews, questioning him about his position with Stuart Vineyards, showing no surprise when she discovered he handled the sales and public relations work. For all his gentleness, Paul had an appealing personality, as well as a wealthy family that carried a lot of influence in this part of California. His weakness lay in his obsession with Alisa, the first thing that neither his money nor his name had been able to buy. Still, he could be quite charming when he wanted to be. And tonight, under Alisa's attentive regard, his bitterness gradually fell away as he responded eagerly to her interest.

From the soup to the salad, through the fish course and the meat course and finally the dessert, Alisa could feel the displeasure emanating from Zachary at her monopolization of Paul. A few times she had smiled rather sweetly at him, asking if he agreed with a statement, then continued without giving Zachary an opportunity to comment. At last Zachary broke in to suggest that they withdraw to the living-room to sample the latest bottle of Muscat produced by his winery. This time when Paul would have escorted Alisa in, Zachary was at her elbow, his sardonic eyes compelling Paul to precede them.

Once in the living-room, Christine hurried to where the big dog lay on the blue Persian rug near the white stone fireplace, sitting herself down beside him. Alisa, with the thought to thwart any attempt at intimacy by Zachary, seated herself in the large cushioned chair near the couch where Paul was seated. But after passing out the petite crystal glasses glimmering with the pale golden wine, Zachary moved to Alisa's chair and rested his lanky frame on the armrest, his arm trailing along the back of the chair so that his hand was in easy reach of the escaping tendrils of hair. They were inseparably joined in Paul's vision so that any remark he made had to be addressed to them both.

Subtly, with Alisa hardly being aware of what was happening, Zachary took charge of the conversation, steering the subject to the winery and the harvest a month away. Even as she turned her cool gaze up to him, her mouth curving at the corners to the bidding of her mind, meeting the brooding anger of his black eyes, she couldn't be sure of his emotion. In that moment as she looked up at him and his two fingers captured a wispy strand of hair in an intimate gesture she knew she hated him, violently and totally. But Zachary only sneered at her when she pulled her head away from his caress, openly mocking her attempt to escape him.

'I think your sister has had a pretty long day. It's time you put her to bed, Alisa,' Zachary said.

Alisa glanced guiltily towards the hearth and the yawning auburn head that was nodding drowsily beside the sleeping German Shepherd. Her concern for her sister forbade her to dispute the commanding tone of his voice as she quickly excused herself to Paul, adding pleasantly that they would see each other often, which brought her another censorious look from her husband.

'After Christine falls asleep, you must come down and join us.' Again there was no invitation, only an order in Zachary's voice.

But Alisa just smiled her false smile of affection while prompting Chris to say good night, happy to leave the room and her husband's suffocating presence.

An hour later, Alisa had bathed Christine, finally persuaded her to change into her pyjamas, and suffered through her endless jabberings about Baron, Zachary's police dog. When the last burst of energy abated, Alisa tucked her into bed, smiling that she would be in the next room and that she would leave the connecting bathroom doors open in case Chris needed her. She had no intention of obeying Zachary's edict that she return downstairs.

If she had to look up once more and see that black hair over those equally dark eyes and that aristocratic nose that succeeded in making her feel that he was regarding her with disdain while his hard, curling mouth jeered at her, Alisa felt she would scream. So instead she removed her pale green top, the white linen skirt over her shorts, and put on her long-sleeved satin housecoat, before busying herself with washing off the light make-up she used. Seated at her lighted dressing-table, she used a little witch hazel to remove the mascara. After applying night cream which gave her lightly tanned skin a golden glow, Alisa unpinned her hair and began brushing it with strong, vigorous strokes.

The electricity crackled through her hair as she bristled inwardly with hatred for the man who was now her husband. He was so arrogantly confident, the epitome of the superior male, that the thought of him sickened her. Even now in the sanctity of her room, Alisa could feel the masculine vitality of his presence surrounding her and stifling her with the force of his will. She tilted her head to the opposite side, her brush attacking her long hair as her eyes strayed to the mirror in front of her, meeting the reflection of a pair of dark, insolent eyes belonging to the tall figure standing just

68

inside her door.

'What are you doing here?' Her tightening lips released her cold, snipped words slowly as Alisa turned to face Zachary.

'You didn't come back downstairs.' How she hated the smooth way he had of putting her on the defensive!

'I didn't choose to,' Alisa replied, resuming the rhythmic strokes of her brush. At his failure to answer, she laid the brush down, pivoting on her bench to face him. 'This is my room. Will you please get out!'

'It's a shame you weren't downstairs.' Calmly Zachary placed a cigarette between his lips and lit it. 'I gave an excellent performance to Paul about my anxious bride waiting upstairs for me. It was quite amusing to see him blanch and hasten to leave.'

'I'm not amused; I'm disgusted.' Alisa retorted viciously. 'Do you steal candy from children, too?'

'What is this?' Zachary laughed. 'A touch of conscience at such a late date? I wasn't the one that drove Paul to swallowing a bottle full of sleeping tablets. You were the one who referred to him as a sweaty-palmed milksop who naturally bungled a suicide attempt, not I! Are you trying to tell me that you would have treated him differently if you'd known?'

Alisa looked away to hide the two bright spots of colour on her cheeks, induced by the twinge of self-disgust at her own callousness.

'I don't know,' she murmured, then more positively, 'No, I wouldn't have treated him differently. But I wasn't as cruel and ruthless as you! Do you know what he thought? He thought that you'd brought me here for him, that you'd persuaded me to give Paul another chance. I've never felt so sorry for anyone as I did Paul when you so blatantly informed him that I was married to you. You could have had the grace to break it to him gently, but instead you flaunted me in his face as if I was some kind of trophy.'

'You're not a trophy; you're a booby prize,' Zachary drawled, deep amusement adding to the mockery in his voice. 'Pampering and pity don't grow backbones, so don't waste them on Paul. If you would have co-operated with me this evening, instead of fighting me, we could have accomplished a great deal.'

'And how would allowing you to paw me accomplish anything for Paul?' Sarcasm and scorn were etched openly on her face as her frosty eyes reproved him.

'I've answered that question earlier in the evening and I don't intend to repeat myself!' Zachary blazed at her, his gaze narrowing on her haughty face threateningly. 'At least you've told me the real reason you didn't come down. You were afraid of me – or more specifically of my making love to you, no matter how innocent it was.'

'That is a lie!' Alisa spat. 'You disgust me and repulse me, but I don't fear you or your sickening display of virility in front of others. We've made a business arrangement. Any ideas that you may have that it will become anything other than that are totally wrong. I loathe the entire male race – and especially you, Mr. Stuart!'

'We've been leading up to this discussion since yesterday,' Zachary shrugged. 'Are you challenging me deliberately, or is it only subconsciously that you want me to make love to you?'

Her tightly controlled temper snapped at his revolting statement. Grabbing her brush as a weapon, Alisa rose from the dressing-table to fling herself at him. Zachary caught the arm brandishing the brush, twisting it until Alisa dropped it with a cry of pain. She struggled, clawing with her free hand at the arm that held hers in a stranglehold. Easily he captured that one, drawing both behind her back where he held them with one hand. At the same time he crushed her to his body.

'I hate you!' she hissed, her words muffled against his chest.

'Do you expect me to believe that?' Zachary chuckled, twisting her chin up so that she was forced to look into his face. 'You knew this would happen when you made that pathetically feminine attack. You knew you'd end up a prisoner in my arms.'

A shiver raced through Alisa as she knew a moment of fear that there might be a bit of truth in his words, but the idea was too preposterous. Anger at his supreme conceit had made her attack him, forgetting his superior strength at the height of her temper.

'You're incredibly vain!' Most of her composure was regained and her words were uttered with her former coolness.

'I can imagine how Petruchio felt when faced with the taming of the shrew Katharina.' At the small sound

71

of contempt that Alisa made, Zachary added, 'I could make you fall in love with me.' With a gesture of disdain, he released her, pushing her away from him. 'But that wasn't part of our bargain. The two hundred thousand was to provide you with my name and my house. There was no provision that I had to take you to my bed as well, was there? Even though it's unquestionably my right as your husband.'

'I would never let you,' Alisa retorted, incensed by his implication that it was all his decision.

'Let's get one thing straight, Alisa.' Zachary was angry now, his eyes blazing with their black fires. 'I don't choose to take you.'

Alisa stiffened at his arrogant assertion. Her mouth opened to emit a cutting reply, only to close at the sound of a small voice on the other side of the room saying accusingly, 'You woke me up!'

'Chris,' Alisa murmured, turning at once to the sleepy pyjama-clad figure.

'How opportune for you!' sneered Zachary, pivoting smartly on his heel and leaving the room.

It was nearly twenty minutes later before Christine was pacified enough to return her head to the pillow and sleep, and Alisa returned to her own bedroom. Sitting on the edge of the purple velvet bedspread, she rubbed her wrists, the soreness brought on by their imprisonment in Zachary's strong hands bringing fresh tremblings of anger to her. With it came the logical and jarring realization that physically he could master her. And though she thanked God that he didn't want her, Alisa knew that her only two weapons were useless against him. The first was her money, of which

Zachary already had a sizeable amount, and the second was her beauty and desirability which could induce men to do her bidding. But Zachary had made it quite clear that she didn't sway him in the slightest.

It was a restless, troublesome night for Alisa.

CHAPTER THREE

Both Christine and Alisa arose late the next morning with Chris bouncing and eager for the new day and impatient at having to wait while Alisa dusted her face with cornsilk powder and applied the light touches of blue eyeshadow and dark brown mascara. In the morning-room, they were pertly informed by the housekeeper that Zachary had arisen at six, which by her very tone indicated disapproval of their late rising. But cereal, juice, and fruit were quickly placed before Christine while Alisa settled for toast and coffee.

The July sun had climbed to its midday position when Christine finally cajoled Alisa to go outside. The shirtwaist dress that Alisa wore had long sleeves. The lightweight cotton material of white background for the printed blue flowers was cool and protected her from over-exposure to the sun. She had learned some time ago that with her pale hair she looked better with only a light golden tan to her skin instead of the coppery brown that most women attempted to obtain, whereas Christine with her auburn hair succeeded in acquiring more freckles in each outing in the sun.

The pair wandered amid the tall oak trees that encircled the house, pausing for a time near the fence that separated them from the vineyards and their nearly indistinguishable rows of grapevines. But Alisa was too preoccupied to fully pay attention to Christine's numerous questions. And at last Christine turned to her own imagination for entertainment, taking twigs and grass to build a tiny house for the little people that lived in the oak grove. Alisa watched the solemn little hands as they carefully constructed the walls and roofs.

With Christine absorbed in her task, Alisa's thoughts were free to wander. Inextricably they were drawn to Zachary. Alisa knew she was attractive. There was no vanity in the knowledge, just common sense. Her beauty should appeal to Zachary. Yet he seemed to admire it and simultaneously to shrug it off. Her wealth and beauty had always been her best assets that had lured a long string of admirers — none of whom she wanted, it was true, but they were there, all under her control. But this volcanically unpredictable man she had married was not.

Last night Alisa had attempted to take a stand, to let him know that she had no intention of obeying his orders. But she had succeeded only in incurring his caustic insults about her own character. And she had been fool enough to lose her poise and her temper. Zachary had been quick to take advantage of both. Remembering the leashed violence with which he had so easily dismissed her attack, Alisa was also forced to recall the effortless way he crushed her against his chest. Any such intimate contact with a man, Alisa had shunned in the past. The few instances when they had occurred could be numbered on one hand. That was why, she told herself, her struggles had weakened when she met the firm rock wall of his body. Her senses had been heightened, making her totally aware of the arms imprisoning her, the masculine scent of his cologne engulfing her, and the way his breath had danced in

75

her hair. But the haunting, seductive softness of his voice when he had said that he could make Alisa fall in love with him had disturbed her the most. At the time Alisa had been able to signify her contempt for such an assertion. Yet the remembrance drifted back.

Zachary had released her immediately after uttering that statement, irritatingly affirming that their marriage was a mockery and would remain that way as long as he chose it to be so. Despite her bold protests to the contrary, Alisa was forced to acknowledge that it was true. And, although she hadn't shown it, she had been frightened. Part of her had longed to cower in the face of his anger. But she had fought for herself too long. Alisa couldn't help wondering what would have happened if Christine hadn't woken to halt the argument that couldn't allow the other to be the victor.

She had definitely underestimated Zachary. The marriage had been her solution to the conditions of her mother's will, a sacrifice of her own principles for the sake of her sister. She had chosen Zachary thinking to bring him under her thumb. But Alisa had failed, miserably. Her wealth was no longer a thing to be held over his head. Her coldness was a thing for him to taunt. Although she had once considered her desirability a weapon, now she was grateful that it held no allure for Zachary. It was apparent that he could be quite ruthless in getting what he wanted. For once she was lucky that he didn't want her – even though one tiny feminine part of her yearned to know why.

Since her coolness couldn't keep him at arms' length and losing her temper only succeeded in arousing his, the only path left for her to take was to avoid him as much as possible. She and Christine would make their own little world, excluding Zachary Stuart. After all, Alisa thought, without fuel, a fire can't burn – or scorch those who come too near.

Relieved by her decision, Alisa turned to watch Chris's fascinating imagination working as she continued building a series of miniature grass homes. A drumming sound carried through the trees, its staccato beat bringing Alisa's eyes to its direction. The sight of a horse and rider looked incongruous through her aperture of barlike trees with their backdrop of duty vines. The petite figure astride the chestnut horse was clearly female, dressed in dark trousers and a sleeveless red top. Someone must have called out to her, because Alisa saw the girl rein her horse in viciously, forcing him to turn at the same time.

Off to the side of one of the buildings housing the winery, Alisa saw Zachary looking cool and quite composed in shirt-sleeves and wheat tan slacks. The horse danced to a halt in front of him as his rider sat stiffly in the saddle. They were too far away for Alisa to hear their conversation, but it was evident that the dark-haired girl was angry, although the arrogant set of Zachary's shoulders indicated that he was unmoved by her. Without warning the girl's hand raised and the quirt in her hand came down with sudden swiftness. Zachary raised an arm to block the blow and with the other grabbed the girl and pulled her out of the saddle. Alisa could see Zachary laugh as his captive struggled uselessly in his arms.

Then there was a moment of stillness. His mouth was moving in speech. Whatever it was that was said Alisa didn't know, but the girl's arms suddenly entwined around his neck as she pulled his head down to hers. Her stomach churned with sickening nausea, yet she was unable to look away from the obviously growing passion of their embrace. At last she shut her eyes, no longer able to stand the abandonment with which the girl gave herself to Zachary.

She hated and despised Zachary Stuart! Her body trembled with the violence of her feelings. He was an animal, a beast! Oh, how she prayed that she would never see him again! How could they be so uncouth as to carry on like that out here in the open where anyone could see them! Alisa glanced quickly at Christine who was still engrossed with her 'little people'. At least she hadn't seen them.

CHAPTER FOUR

AT lunchtime, Nora informed Christine and Alisa that Zachary would not be joining them. Sandwiches were being sent up to him at the winery. Although Christine expressed disappointment, Alisa could barely hide her relief at not being forced to sit at the same table with him. Her vow to avoid him was renewed with vigour.

By dinnertime that evening, her barriers were firmly in place, only to have the satisfaction taken away by the paper wall of the *San Francisco Chronicle* that Zachary erected between them. Rising from the table after dessert had been served, Zachary excused himself, stating that he had bookwork to catch up on, then sarcastically adding that he was sure Alisa didn't object to entertaining herself. She had no alternative but to agree, much as it galled her that he was the one to do the suggesting and not herself.

The pattern continued for five days, with Zachary always taking the initiative to insure that Alisa was the one who was left alone. Never once did Zachary use the den for his work, always leaving the house to walk towards the winery. Alisa couldn't help assuming that he was keeping an assignation with the rider of the horse.

The fifth night it began raining shortly after Zachary had left. The entire day had been threatening with a heavy cloud cover, which had finally released its burden. Alisa was curled up on the couch trying to convince herself that the book she was reading was interesting. But after four previous nights of only a book for company, she was becoming bored. And the steady beat of the rain outside made her restless. Snapping the lighter to her cigarette, she laid the book down and studied the smear of her lipstick on the filter tip.

The telephone rang sharply in the still room, momentarily startling Alisa with its harshness. She waited, expecting Nora to answer the hallway phone before she remembered that the housekeeper had already returned to her home on the grounds, formerly a coach house. Alisa picked up the receiver of the living-room extension just before the third ring. Just as she started to speak she heard Zachary's voice announce, 'Stuart Vineyards.'

'Did you order this rain, Zach?' the woman's voice was teasing with a sensuous huskiness to it.

'No, I didn't,' Zachary replied. There was a slight pause. 'Excuse me, Renée, I think someone else is on the line. I have the phone. You can hang up now.'

Alisa inhaled sharply at his sarcastic tone and slammed the receiver down, hoping it would break their eardrums. He had to have known it was she on the other end. No one else was in the house except Christine, who was already in bed. There he was having an affair with another woman and he had the nerve to imply that she, Alisa, was behaving improperly! At least, she thought smugly, the rain dampened this evening's rendezvous.

The sun finally came out again late in the afternoon of

the following day. The gentle breeze carried with it the salty tang of the Pacific Ocean. Alisa watched the contented figure of her half-sister busily administering to the needs of her doll, which had arrived with the rest of her things the day before. A little sigh escaped the bronze-tinged lips as Alisa wished for the serenity of the child.

It was a consolation to know that Chris was happy, since that had been the whole purpose of this marriage. Alisa loved Chris dearly and didn't begrudge the sacrifice she had made. But she had never felt so bored, restless and frustrated in all her life. What was more irritating was the fact that she was the only one that felt that way! If only Zachary did too, here would at least be some feeling of achievement. As Alisa had found out last night, he was already quite happily engaged in other diversions, while she sat alone in the house playing the part of a dutiful wife.

The housekeeper, Nora, was still barely civil towards her. And Alisa wasn't about to associate with the short-tempered cook, although she knew that Christine came and went out of the kitchen whenever she pleased. Zachary rose and was gone from the house before Alisa awoke. Again Christine invariably breakfasted with him before she went to waken her sister. There was no one for Alisa to associate with, and as much as she loved her little sister, Chris couldn't provide the adult companionship that Alisa wanted.

'Nora said you were out here. May I join you?' a masculine voice asked from the veranda door of the house.

Alisa rose quickly at the voice. 'Paul!' she cried,

stretching out her hands in relief and welcome. 'It's so good to see you again. Do come on out.'

In that brief second when she recognized him, two different emotions waved through her. One that she was glad she had worn her white slacks that hugged her hips before clinging to her thighs, then belling out around her ankles, and the sky blue midriff top that matched her eyes. She knew the outfit was vastly becoming to her. The second feeling was that Paul had changed. Perhaps it was the air of confidence that enhanced his natural attractiveness.

Now, as he stepped forward to take one of her hands, Alisa noticed the ribboned gift in his other arm. She quickly drew him over to a chair near hers and sat down, offering him a glass of iced tea from the pitcher that sat on the glass-topped table beside her.

'I wasn't too sure how welcome you'd be to see me,' Paul said, accepting the frosted glass, a warm and endearing smile on his face. 'Especially after the terrible fool I made of myself the last time. I must have embarrassed you.'

'I was only embarrassed for you and a little angry with Zachary for not letting me know you were here.' A glitter appeared in her eyes in the memory of that evening.

'I brought you a wedding gift.' At the beginning of Alisa's protest, Paul inserted, 'It was the least I could do. You can open it now or you can wait for Zachary, whichever you want.'

A wedding gift – a chill went through Alisa at the thought that their mockery was going a step further. But she managed to smile and assert that she would open it now. When she unwrapped the gift and sifted through the protective confetti, she found the most exquisite set of Steuben crystal wine glasses. She had no difficulty complimenting their beauty, although she did hesitate to assure him of their appropriateness. They were very appropriate for the new bride and bridegroom of Stuart Vineyard, but she just disliked the linking of Zachary and herself even by a wedding gift.

'I know this probably sounds strange to you,' Paul said, 'but since I couldn't have you, I'm glad you married Zachary. Our families have been friends for years. I don't know of anyone who doesn't admire and respect him.' Alisa longed to correct Paul and say there was one who didn't, but she kept her silence. 'I can see that marriage has agreed with you already. You're not so aloof as you once were. There's a warmness and compassion about you that wasn't there before.'

Had she changed? Alisa wondered. Compassionate – yes, she was. Once she had been impervious to Paul's feelings, uncaring of whether he had been hurt or not. Now she did care. Part of her saw him as a child much like Christine. Why hadn't she noticed this unselfish side to Paul? She had been so quick to condemn him before, to laugh at his pathetic declarations of love. But now her conscience asked if it were his declarations that were pathetic or her reaction. Alisa refused to consider the question. For the moment it was enough to realize that Paul was a true friend, the first one who had ever wanted nothing more except her happiness.

With a sincerity that surprised even Alisa, she set out to question him about his home, his family, his life, marvelling at the pride in his voice when he spoke so lovingly about his parents or so earnestly about his position at the vineyard. Chris was the one who finally broke into the discussion, tiring of playing by herself and with touching innocence enlisting Paul and Alisa into a game of 'keep-away' with her big yellow ball.

Twice Alisa found herself laughing at Paul's exaggerated attempts to keep the ball from being tossed past him. She couldn't honestly remember the last time she had laughed in the company of an adult, not even Michael. At last Paul intercepted the ball and it was Christine's turn to be in the centre. With a sense of elation, Alisa knew this was the way she had always imagined a family would be. As she took her turn in the centre, Alisa managed a hesitant smile of gratitude at Paul, hardly knowing that the animated glow on her face was a breathtaking change from the supremely poised expression that Paul was accustomed to seeing. Chris tossed the ball high over Alisa's head, laughing delightedly when her older sister jumped in the air after it. Coming down, Alisa's sandals slipped on the wet grass. She would have fallen if Paul hadn't grabbed her by the waist and steadied her on to her feet.

She had turned her ankle on landing and there was a spasm of protesting pain when she tried to put her weight on it. Paul immediately insisted on helping her to a chair, then kneeling on the patio to inspect her foot.

'I only turned it, Paul,' Alisa protested, but a warmth went through her at his worried frown that silently betrayed his concern that she might have done some serious injury to herself. His solicitude was contagious and Christine hurried to fetch Alisa her cigarettes and her glass of iced tea – anything to make up for the unintentional hurt of her sister.

As much as the fussing pleased her, Alisa finally insisted on standing, compelled to show them that she wasn't seriously injured. Paul's hand remained firmly on her arm as she walked without limping to the other side of the patio and back.

'You see, I'm fine. It only hurt for a moment after I turned it,' she said, arriving back at her starting point.

'You gave me a start.' Paul shook his head in relief. 'We'd better call off the games for a while, Chris. That grass is too slippery. The next time someone just might get really hurt.'

Chris agreed, then went off bouncing the ball vigorously over the patio announcing that she was going to count to see how long she could keep it bouncing. Paul and Alisa watched her silently for a time before Paul finally rose to his feet.

'I'd better be going, Alisa. I didn't intend to stay this long.'

'I'm glad you came, and I hope you come often,' Alisa returned, for the first time meaning every word she said.

'Not too often,' Paul smiled. 'I'd hate to make Zach jealous.'

'Who cares what he thinks!' Hiding the biting tone with a smile, 'Chris and I would love to have you here any time. I'll walk you to your car so you can be sure my ankle is completely unhurt.

Paul protested, but Alisa could tell it was only half-hearted. At the edge of the drive, Paul insisted that she go no farther, asserting that there was no need for her to muddy her sandals while dodging the standing puddles of water in the gravelled drive. He took her hand as he bade her good-bye and held it longer than was really necessary, but Alisa didn't mind. Afterwards when he had driven off, waving to her and the distant Christine, Alisa couldn't even remember whether or not his hands had been sweaty as she had once claimed. That distasteful picture of him had been erased from her mind with the new image of him she had acquired today. She stood for several minutes by the drive watching the car as it drove down the tree-lined lane until it disappeared from sight.

'That was a very touching little scene.'

The contented expression on her face froze as Alisa turned her head just far enough to the side to see Zachary standing behind her. There was an underlying current of anger in his voice that said his words were more than idle comment. Even though Paul's car was out of sight, Alisa returned her gaze to the road.

'You should have sent someone to let me know he was here,' Zachary continued.

This time Alisa turned around, staring coldly up into his dark face. 'I don't think he came to see you.'

His eyes glittered encountering the triumphantly aloof expression.

'What did he come for?'

'I believe he came to apologize for embarrassing me the last time he was here,' Alisa replied smoothly, deriving a peculiar enjoyment out of the way Zachary's eyebrows raised in displeasure.

'How long did it take him to make his apologies?'

'About an hour.' Her blue eyes shimmered with defiance.

'I thought I'd made it quite clear to you that I didn't want you encouraging him. I should have thought you'd have done enough damage the last time without leading him to believe that you want his attentions even now that you're married. Haven't you done enough harm to him?' Zachary blazed, his tallness looming over her in intimidation.

'I did absolutely nothing to encourage him to believe I wanted anything other than his friendship,' Alisa replied sharply. 'I had a very enjoyable afternoon in very pleasant company.'

'A man and a woman can never be friends. They're either acquaintances or lovers, but the platonic state you're referring to could never be possible between two normal healthy members of the opposite sex.' Anger smouldered in his gaze while his barbed tongue lashed her unmercifully. 'You may not be experienced enough yet to know that fact, but you'd better accept it as truth, because as long as you're my wife, I don't intend your relationship with Paul to extend any further than an acquaintance!'

'The mighty lord and master has spoken,' Alisa announced scornfully. 'And just how am I supposed to view your relationship with Renée? Are you just acquaintances, or lovers?'

'I wondered how long it would take before you brought that up.' His anger was momentarily shelved to make way for his mocking amusement. 'Surely you remember that I made it very clear that I had no intention of being faithful. I knew the ice maiden I married had enough chastity for both of us.'

'You didn't think I would condone an affair being carried on right beneath my nose, did you? I knew what kind of man you were. The only thing I asked was that you would be discreet. But you can't even do that!'

'You don't know what you're talking about, Alisa. I would advise you to end this conversation now before you push me too far.' His words were spoken concisely as if he were exercising the most extreme control.

'What do you think I am, some dumb blonde who can't see or hear or add up what she does see?' She ignored his warning look. 'Can you deny that you were seen kissing Renée quite thoroughly near the winery buildings? I understood that you usually do your bookwork at the house. What changed your routine?'

'That's quite enough, Alisa!'

'Is it? And just how do you propose to shut me up?'

The speculative gleam that danced within his fiery gaze frightened Alisa a little, but outwardly she didn't change her smug expression.

'I think you'd like me to force myself on you so you can convince yourself all those horrible things you've been thinking about me are true.' His eyes flicked over her defiant stance in a slightly cynical amusement. 'You also know I'm not about to turn the other cheek. You're full of too much pride and too much self-importance. What you need is to be taken down a peg or two.'

Alisa swallowed nervously, trying to shake the feeling that she was watching a jungle cat just before it leaped for its prey. She started to turn to walk away so that he would be left with his threat dangling in the air. But her wrist was pinioned in his vicelike grip. When her other hand tried to rescue the first, it too was captured. For a minute she allowed herself to be his captive, attempting to lull him into a sense of security. Even as she did so, she was bracing herself so that the moment he relaxed she could twist her wrists free.

The moment came. Alisa could feel the slight loosening of his hold. Immediately she tried to pull away, stumbling backward a step or two as she seemed to succeed. Then his grip tightened and she used all her strength to tear away from it. Just as she was beginning to think she wouldn't succeed, Zachary let go. Between the suddenness of his release and the strength with which she was trying to pull away, Alisa lost her balance and fell, sandals, white slacks, bare midriff and all, right into the largest mud puddle in the driveway.

'I could kill you for this, Zachary Stuart!' she cried in a helpless rage as she stared down at her mud-soaked slacks and at the same time tried to shake the gooey earth paste off her hands. Zachary merely looked down at her with the most infuriating smile of satisfaction.

She slipped twice trying to get to her feet, each time glaring up at Zachary for his failure to help her out. By the time she got out of the puddle and had walked with mud squishing through her toes on to the lawn, Christine was standing beside Zachary regarding her mud-drenched sister with open-mouthed surprise.

'At the rear of the house next to the kitchen is a utility room with a shower. You can clean up there,' Zachary told her with maddening amusement.

'What happened?' Christine whispered. But the glaring look from her sister told her quite plainly that she wasn't going to get an answer.

Alisa stalked angrily to the house, aware of Zachary and Christine following her at a respectful distance. She could hear her younger sister giggling and Zachary's laughing voice admonishing her. Briefly she contemplated going through the front door and tracking mud across the polished tile floor, but she couldn't bring herself to do that, no matter how much she wanted to get back at Zachary for humiliating her so. Instead she walked to the rear entrance. She was immediately met by Nora, who stared at her in horror.

'Would you please direct me to the utility room so I can clean up?' Alisa squared her shoulders with all the dignity she could. 'And see to it I have some towels, too. Then go up to my room and get my lavender caftan and some slippers.'

Nora nodded silently, led her through the kitchen to the small room, then left, still staring at Alisa incredulously. Minutes later she was back, bringing snow-white towels and a flannel. Alisa had just decided that there was no way she could pull the mud-covered midriff top off without getting the mud in her hair too, when Christine walked into the room.

'Zach said you'd need some shampoo,' covering her mouth quickly to stifle the giggle that kept trying to bubble through her voice.

'Christine, so help me . . .' Alisa trailed off threateningly.

'I can't help it. You look so funny!' This time she laughed in earnest.

Alisa looked down at her once white slacks, the peculiar chocolate brown paste on her bare waist, and the splattering of mud on her blue top. With a resigned smile, she had to admit that she probably did look quite funny.

'All right – out, you little scamp!' She finally managed to speak in a more understanding voice. 'I've got to get undressed before this stuff hardens on me.'

Christine succumbed to one more burst of giggles before she left the room. Alisa undressed swiftly, adjusted the water temperature, then stepped under the shower. She was busy towelling her long hair to a state of damp dryness when Chris reappeared in the room.

'I'm supposed to tell you that dinner is ready just as soon as you're through. Zachary said you didn't need to worry about how you're dressed because it would just be a simple meal.'

Alisa said she would be out in a few minutes and that Christine should pass the information along. The door had barely shut behind her sister when Alisa again started whispering a few choice descriptive words about Zachary Stuart.

So I needn't bother fussing over my appearance, she thought bitterly. Not that he has ever much cared what I look like. Let's just see what he thinks of wet hair dripping all over his dinner!

She unwrapped the terry towel that had covered her

and slipped on her underclothes and the lavender print caftan. Hurriedly she combed out the tangles of her golden hair, parting it in the centre so that it fell freely to below her shoulders. Slipping on her white thongs, Alisa decided to forgo any lipstick or mascara or other cosmetics. After all, the great lord and master awaited.

Arriving in the dining-room, Alisa was informed by the housekeeper that dinner would be served on the patio that evening. She was just about to open the patio door when she looked out to see Zachary bending beside Chris's doll's pram attempting to fix a wobbly wheel. It was a curious thing to watch this earthy man displaying such concentration over a childish contraption. When it was fixed, he hoisted Christine on his shoulder and was duly rewarded with a kiss.

Alisa made a production out of rattling the door-knob, her feet clattering on the cement patio, and the door shutting a little louder than was necessary. But if she had hoped to break up the intimate scene she had just witnessed, she was mistaken. When she had at last focused her attention on the pair, Christine was still held in Zachary's arms and they were both looking at her with ill-concealed amusement. Alisa regarded Zachary coldly.

'Your sister's here. Looks like we're ready to eat, Peanut,' he jested to Chris, slowly setting her to the ground.

'Why do you call me Peanut?' Chris demanded, bending her head way back so that she could look up to his face.

'Because you're about the size of one and you're as

nutty as one.' Zachary ruffled her hair affectionately. 'Your menu is courtesy of little sister tonight,' addressing Alisa. 'Hamburgers, french fries, cole slaw, cokes, and ice cream for dessert. A cuisine that would turn the palate of any gourmet!'

'And we have pickles, ketchup, mustard, onions, tomatoes, cheese, just everything to put on hamburgers. Come and see, Lisa,' Christine tugged Alisa's stiffened arm impatiently.

Alisa met Zachary's mocking gaze which told her clearly that she looked unharmed by her unglamorous fall into the mud puddle. She longed to tell him how ungentlemanly he was, except that she knew such a statement would be met with amused contempt. Instead Alisa assumed a bland air of unconcern, allowing herself to be drawn to the patio table by Christine and her innocent, festive air. As long as her attention was averted from Zachary and concentrated on Chris, Alisa found she could enjoy the meal. Eventually, once Christine's appetite was satisfied, she hurried off to wheel her newly repaired doll's pram around the house. And Alisa was left with Zachary for company.

The evening sun cast long shadows. Those from the tall oaks gently stretched over the pair. Zachary silently offered Alisa a cigarette, lit hers and then one for himself. The breeze had died until there was only the merest-tickling of movement in the air. Distantly to their ears came the trilling of birds singing the nightcalls to them. All the strain and anger that had filled Alisa was strangely whisked away by the hush of nightfall.

'These lazy summer evenings are the most peaceful

times of all,' Zachary mused softly. His onyx dark eyes glanced swiftly at Alisa as if apologizing for breaking the stillness. 'It's the time you rest up before the harvest season. Once you've been here at harvest time, it's hard to believe it was ever as serene as it is this evening.'

'You're a strange man,' Alisa murmured.

'Am I?' This time his gaze settled on her face, mocking, inspecting, and yet somehow Alisa got the feeling that he was interested in her answer.

'You don't seem like the kind of man who would own or operate a vineyard except as a hobby that you could indulge in whenever it suited your mood.'

'What kind of man do you believe I am?' This time he studied the white puffs of smoke curling from the end of his cigarette.

'I see you as an entrepreneur, a speculator, involved in wheeling and dealing, and manipulating others to do your bidding. The image of you as a vintner doesn't seem right. I just can't picture you being dictated to by the sun and the wind and the weather. Why didn't you follow in your father's footsteps, pick up where he left off?'

'Yes, my father was an important, powerful man. What you don't know is that it was my mother's wish that he be that way. His happiest times were spent here at Stuart Vineyard. It was a rundown, shabby place when he bought it. His dream was to make its wine nationally renowned. There is no lasting joy in dominating other people, but the challenge of Mother Nature is profoundingly enduring.' Zachary smiled a twisting smile of an adult to a child, of one who knows to one who is learning.

'Then why do you try to dominate me?' she thrust, irritated by his knowing attitude.

'All I'm doing is seeing to it that you don't dominate me.' He spoke smoothly, without any suggestion of rancour in his voice. 'And you do try, so pathetically hard, Alisa.'

Seized by a restlessness brought on by his subtly probing gaze, Alisa rose and walked to where a spreading oak tree stood at the edge of the patio. Yes, she was always testing, trying to see if he would allow her to dominate him. If he would be as weak as the others and cater to her needs. She stared at the purple sky infused with a brilliant fuchsia pink, aware that Zachary had risen, too, and had halted a few steps away from her. She turned her troubled blue eyes towards him.

'You look curiously vulnerable right now,' Zachary said. 'Not much older than Christine, with your hair tumbling over your shoulders and your face scrubbed clean of make-up peculiar to the female artifice.'

Alisa did feel vulnerable. She didn't know how to handle this gentleness that Zachary was displaying. It frightened her, the way some of her defences were breaking down. She turned her back to him and stared into the sky at the silvery slip of moon that hung so precariously.

'You try so hard to be independent and strong.' His hands slipped under her hair and began gently massaging the tense muscles in her neck. 'You pile your hair on top of your head, cover your face with sophisticated cosmetics and wrap your heart in coldness. You've taken the world on your shoulders.' His voice was a soft, caressing whisper that was oddly soothing and hypnotic. 'You've made Chris your sole responsibility and refuse help from everyone. Haven't you ever wanted anyone to take care of *you*?'

As much as she wanted to, Alisa couldn't admit to him any such feeling. Instead she came as close as she could to saying the same thing. 'I've often wondered what my father was like. If he was kind and gentle, or strong and powerful ...' She paused. 'I was only a child when he died, and my mother remarried so many times after that.' She wasn't aware of the slight drooping of her shoulders or the fact that she was resting against Zachary's broad chest. His hands had moved to knead the upper portion of her arms.

The languid summer night, the tender massage of Zachary's hands, and the soft, gentle murmur of his voice combined to drift Alisa away into a world partly made up of the reality of the warmth of his hands on her and the lure of security and safety for a father she had never known. How wonderful it would be to have a father you belonged to, to know that he would always be there whenever you needed him, Alisa thought, to be loved just for yourself, not because you were beautiful or talented or rich.

'Come out of your dream world, Alisa. Your father was no paragon of virtue.' His voice, though still soft, sounded harsh in the still air. 'Every human being's feet are made of clay. Your father could have been one of the world's all-time losers.'

'How can you say that!' Alisa cried, springing forward to be free of his hands while turning to see his face. 'You didn't know him! You didn't know what he was like!'

'Neither did you.' Zachary studied her with a hard and thoughtful gaze. 'You're a beautiful and desirable woman. I just want to be sure you don't get a man's attentions confused with fatherly affection. There's not a man made who could look at you and have paternal concern on his mind, including myself.'

'You're a pompous, arrogant . . . !' Alisa spluttered. 'I didn't get to be twenty-four years old without learning that lesson!'

'I'm glad. I'd hate to see you get your dreams mixed up with reality.'

'Zach, there's a phone call for you!' Nora called from the house.

'That must be Renée. Did you miss another rendezvous?' Alisa asked spitefully.

'I told you once that you didn't know what you're talking about. But since you don't choose to believe me, I insist that you keep your opinions to yourself!' His eyes flashed fiery warning signals at her which she shrugged off aloofly. Zachary hesitated as if to argue the point with her, before finally turning sharply on his heel to the house.

Zachary returned a few minutes later to inform Alisa that the phone call had been from his mother. He added, sarcastically, that his mother would be driving from San Francisco to have dinner with them a week from Sunday and to meet his wife. After relaying his message, Zachary started to leave. Inadvertently Alisa asked where he was going.

He looked her up and down thoughtfully. 'I'll be back later this evening,' was his only reply.

It was nearly one o'clock in the morning before Alisa heard the car pull into the driveway and she knew that Zachary had returned. Sleep had escaped her. The books she had picked up couldn't hold her attention. Finally she had just lain in bed waiting subconsciously for her husband to return. Only after she had heard him come up the stairs, the sound of his bedroom door opening and closing, did she finally turn over in her bed and fall into a heavy, dreamless sleep.

That following week Christine had been cranky and out of sorts, demanding more and more from Alisa. Several times she slipped away, going up to the winery in spite of orders from Alisa to the contrary. But Christine had ignored the scoldings, regaling Alisa with tales of men taking the temperature of the wines, sipping out of different glasses and talking about what the wine tasted like. Alisa silently envied her sister's escapades, but she couldn't find the way to halt her wanderings or curb Chris's headstrong and precocious attitudes.

One evening Zachary had finally stepped in and ordered Christine to bed. Alisa had stood silently by while Chris stomped up the stairs before Alisa flew at Zachary in a rage. But he had been adamant. If Alisa couldn't discipline the child then he would. And he had no intention of letting a seven-year-old child rule his house with her whining and tantrums.

Alisa had known he was right, although she absolutely refused to admit it. She had pampered Christine too much, trying to make sure she didn't miss her parents more than was necessary. Zachary had dismissed her sentimentality, saying that children were more resilient than adults and could adjust quicker to a change in their environment. What had been harder to take was Christine's attitude. Alisa had gone up to her bedroom when her argument with Zachary had reached a stalemate. Christine had got ready for bed and was busy saying her prayers. After her usual 'God bless Mommy and Dad who are in heaven and tell them I love them,' came 'God bless Alisa and God bless Zach.' It was the first time Alisa had ever heard her include Zachary's name in her prayers.

Gently, trying to hide her curiosity, Alisa had asked, 'Aren't you angry with Zachary any more?'

'No. I wasn't angry with him before. I just wondered if he put up with me because of you, or whether he really liked me,' the auburn-haired child replied sagaciously. 'Now I know he likes me.'

'How? Because he ordered you to your room?' Alisa frowned.

'Yes.' The simple statement was accompanied by a wide smile as she crawled under the covers of her bed. 'You only yell and get mad at the people you like.'

With that explanation Alisa had to be satisfied. Although it was contradictory, it made sense. But it also made her wonder if she should delve into her own feelings on the subject, something she was loath to do.

Alisa had difficulty making up her mind what to wear to the dinner with Zachary's mother. After removing half the clothes from her closet, she finally decided on a featherlight crêpe suit of ivory tan with a bright red and gold silk blouse in a paisley print. As she was adjusting the collar, a knock came at her bedroom door. Impatiently she called out permission to enter, thinking it was Christine again, who was not looking forward to the day at all. But it was Zachary.

'I just suggested to Chris that she eat in the kitchen with Nora,' he said, looking very impressive in a summer weight suit of light brown. 'She isn't quite old enough to be included in an adult dinner.'

'She'll be happy about that,' Alisa replied, ignoring his gaze that sought hers in the mirror.

He walked slowly across the room to lean against the wall beside Alisa's dressing-table. Reaching into his coat pocket, he withdrew a small black box, flipped it open and removed the ring inside. He reached down and clasped her left hand, slipping the ring on her finger.

'They'll expect to see something other than the gold band,' he said in answer to Alisa's surprised glance. A deep red ruby gleamed brilliantly at her from its setting encircled with diamonds. 'A blue sapphire would have more suited your nature,' sarcasm in his voice, 'but I chose to include the fire you lack in the ring.'

'It's very beautiful.' Her eyes glimmered coolly up to his. 'But you didn't have to go to this extreme just to keep up appearances.'

'You don't believe I spent my money for this?' he mocked.

Alisa ignored his taunt, her mind flitting back to his first statement that 'they' would be expecting a ring. 'What did you mean when you said "they" would be expecting me to wear a ring?'

'Didn't I tell you? Mother is staying with the Gautiers. I decided that we might as well have them over as well. They're our nearest neighbours. This dinner will stave off any further need for a get-acquainted party in the future.' His eyebrows raised as if Zachary was surprised by her question. Then he smiled. 'I invited Paul and your cousin Michael, too, which should make you happy.'

'It's so thoughtful of you to inform me of this ahead of time.' With jerky, angered movements, Alisa picked up her lipstick case and reapplied the mocha tint to her lips. 'I hope you don't intend to subject our guests to any of your contrived, intimate scenes.'

'Let's just say that as long as you appear the model wife, I'll be the model husband, solicitous, but not overly affectionate.'

Alisa glared coldly at his jeering expression as she rose from the dressing-table and walked to the bed to slip on the matching jacket to her skirt.

'What time is this entourage supposed to arrive?' she asked.

Zachary glanced at his wristwatch. 'In about a half hour to an hour. Are you coming downstairs to welcome them with me, or are you planning a grand entrance after they've arrived?'

Stiffened momentarily at his biting sarcasm, Alisa finally turned to smile maliciously, 'I'll be at my husband's side, of course.'

'I'm glad you said that,' smiling that lazy smile that never ceased to remind Alisa of a Cheshire cat. 'I wouldn't have liked to start an argument by insisting on it.'

Michael was the first to arrive, gazing at the decor in open assessment. He was a bit overawed by Zachary, which didn't dim his curiosity a bit. It only gave him a sort of furtive air. Taking a glass of sherry from Alisa, he winked and whispered, 'How's the old married lady doing? You've got quite a handful with him, don't you think?'

Alisa had laughed off his 'I-told-you-so' smirk with ease, hoping to shatter Michael's assumption that the war was tilting in Zachary's favour. Zachary answered the door alone when the second bell rang to announce the arrival of Paul. He was escorted into the living-room where Alisa and Michael were seated. By the time Zachary had given him a glass of sherry, the bell rang again. This time it was several minutes before he returned to the room. Alisa hid her nervousness behind a bright smile as an older couple entered the room. The man was slender, of medium height, with a distinguishing touch of white hair at his temples amidst an abundance of dark curling hair. The woman on his arm wore a dark blue dress which was very becoming despite her plumpness. Her hair, too, was very dark, but it was streaked throughout with grey which her coiffure accented.

Behind them walked Zachary. The woman on his right was the first to come into Alisa's view. She was very petite and slender, dressed in an elegant pink chiffon dress that strangely complemented her chestnut brown hair. Only when she stepped closer could Alisa see the betraying lines of age around her eyes and neck. Zachary had begun the introductions of Louis and Estelle Gautier when Alisa saw the girl on the other side of him, whom he drew forward gently to include her as the daughter of the Gautiers, Renée.

Alisa knew a chill had come over her features as she extended her hand to the girl. But it was mild in comparison to the glaring hatred in the brown eyes looking back at her. Alisa couldn't help studying this girl who met secretly with her husband. Her hair was long and black; she was easily four inches shorter than Alisa, slender though still with provocative curves well displayed in a tangerine silk dress. Her lashes were naturally long and thick and framed large wide eyes that now stared at Alisa hostilely. The heart-shaped face contained a widow's peak on the smooth forehead, a button nose to match her petiteness, and full, sensuous lips outlined in an orange-red to match her dress. At last, after Renée had murmured with false enthusiasm how pleased she was to meet Zachary's new wife, Zachary stepped forward with his mother.

His eyes travelled mockingly over Alisa's frozen expression even as he introduced his mother. There was interest but no friendliness in Mrs. Stuart's face as she greeted Alisa. In fact, Alisa got the impression that the woman didn't like what she saw.

'I've looked forward to meeting you, Mrs. Stuart,' Alisa managed to say politely. She was intensely aware that Michael had witnessed the interchange of hostilities between her and Renée and was amused. He was also very anxious to find a place beside Renée.

'And I've wanted to meet you, the girl who managed to spirit my son away without any advance notice.' Mrs. Stuart laughed a tinkling, teasing laugh that made Alisa feel uncomfortable. 'Of course, he knew I always planned for him to have such a big wedding. And you know how men are about such functions;

they're always so anxious to get them over with. Zachary, bring me some of your sherry. Then run along and talk about your winery with Louis as you always do.'

Zachary nodded his obedience and moved away. Alisa knew where her husband acquired such a dominating air, especially when Mrs. Stuart insisted that they sit down and get to know one another. Zachary returned with the sherry, waited while his mother sipped it, commenting, 'It's very good, darling,' then he seated himself in a chair next to Louis Gautier and Paul. Alisa was quick to note that Renée had draped herself on the arm of her father's chair nearest to Zachary. Her blue eyes glanced frostily at Zachary, who smiled wickedly back before turning to speak to Louis. Michael was busy trying to engage Renée's attention, without much success.

'I understand you have a daughter,' Mrs. Stuart drew her attention back.

'A daughter? No, my little sister, Christine, is living with us,' Alisa corrected. 'Our parents are both dead.'

'Oh, how unfortunate for Zachary.' She smiled with solicitous sweetness at Alisa. 'And for you, too, my dear. I just meant that it was too bad that you two had to start out with family responsibilities immediately.'

'Christine has a trust fund, so she's really not a financial liability to us,' Alisa retorted a little more sharply than she intended.

'Who has control of this trust fund?'

'I do,' Alisa replied coolly.

'That's good. Sometimes lawyers and bankers can be so insensitive to the needs of a child, if you know what I mean.' Zachary's mother's smile was so ingratiatingly coy that Alisa had to grit her teeth to keep from making a sarcastic remark. 'It was such a shock to me when Zachary called to tell me he was married. I wasn't even aware he knew you. Now that I've met you I can see why you entranced him so. You're very beautiful.'

'Thank you. That's a very nice compliment for a mother-in-law to make.' The words practically choked her even as Alisa said them.

'You're not entirely the type of person that I expected Zachary to choose. I always imagined that he would pick someone with dark hair and eyes, like himself. Of course your paleness is a perfect foil for him, but I've always thought similar couples are so much more striking. Now you and Paul would look so good together, with you both being so fair.' The raised voice brought Zachary's gaze narrowing down on Alisa. The conversation was growing increasingly unbearable for Alisa and a severe strain to her manners. Mrs. Stuart smiled at her in a confiding yet apologetic way. 'I must confess that the Gautiers and I always felt that Renée and Zachary would marry. It would have been so ideal, you know. The vineyards join one another to the north. And the Gautiers are such a respected and renowned name in California. Poor Louis is getting so much older and he only has Renée to inherit his holdings. For a time, she and Zachary seemed very fond of one another; marriage seemed the obvious step for both of them, which would have pleased both our families. But of course, that was before he met you, dear.'

Alisa wondered what Mrs. Stuart's reaction would be if she learned that her son and Renée were still quite fond of each other, and what would she think if she found out that Zachary had married Alisa for the sum of two hundred thousand dollars? It would probably make no difference, Alisa decided, since she had the impression that Mrs. Stuart was motivated by social position and not money.

'I believe I've made Zachary quite happy in the short time of our marriage,' Alisa commented, knowing of no other statement she could make in the face of Mrs. Stuart's obvious preference for a different daughter-in-law.

'I'm sure you have.' The woman patted Alisa's hand in dubious affection. 'I just wish I could have met you sooner, but my son was insistent that you two should have time together alone before you met his dragon of a mother.' Again the tinkling laughter.

Unconsciously Alisa reached for a cigarette and held the lighter to it with her left hand. Her ruby ring flashed the reflection of the flame brightly.

'Oh, is that your ring!' Mrs Stuart exclaimed. 'Such exquisite taste my son has.'

'Let me see it!' Renée rose from the arm of her father's chair with a flourish, moving gracefully across the small space to where Alisa and Mrs. Stuart were seated. Her delicate hand caught hold of Alisa's as she raised it higher to see the ring more clearly. 'A ruby!' she cried, casting the amused Zachary a teasing glance. 'It's my favourite stone!'

Alisa had an unaccountable urge to tear the ring off her finger and hand it to the girl. Instead she smiled and thanked Renée politely, meeting Zachary's eyes for a moment before he turned his gaze to Paul who was addressing him.

'How strange that Zach would pick a ruby for your engagement ring,' Renée was saying with lilting huskiness to her voice. 'It hardly suits you. Diamonds or sapphires would seem to be more in your order.' The malevolent gleam was back in her dark eyes.

'There have been misconceptions by other people before regarding what suits me, but they've been invariably wrong.' Alisa held back none of the sarcasm in her tone as she met the brown eyes with a frosty glare of her own. If Renée wanted to do battle, Alisa decided that she might as well know she had a formidable opponent.

'Mother, Alisa,' Zachary interrupted. 'Dinner is ready.' He offered an arm to each, smiling down at Alisa in what probably seemed to most an amiable smile, but Alisa saw the warning look that was meant strictly for her.

Zachary was seated at the head of the table with Alisa at the opposite end. Alisa was happy to see his mother seated to his left. Now she wouldn't have to tolerate any more of Mrs. Stuart's offensively kind remarks. She was rather surprised to discover that she was upset by the fact that Renée was on Zachary's right, her dark brown eyes already flirting outrageously at him. Michael was to Renée's right, trying to compete with Zachary as the centre of her attention. Alisa was able to quell the brief rise of anger by turning to Louis Gautier and his wife, who were sitting on each side of her. Mrs. Gautier was a very self-effacing woman, referring any opinions to her husband. Her excessive politeness and soothing manner greatly eased Alisa's tension. Paul was between the two older women, as usual charming both of them.

As the meal progressed, Alisa became more and more conscious of deliberately avoiding any glances towards the opposite end of the table. But she couldn't stop hearing Zachary's voice, so low and so musical as he replied to Renée's questioning. There was no mockery, no amusement in his tone, only charm and interest. It was such a vast difference from their own conversations that always held an underlying air of jeering dislike.

When the main course of roast rack of lamb arrived, Zachary poured a glass of rosé wine for each guest. Louis held his up to the light, studied it, smelled it, sipped it, then nodded approvingly to Zachary.

'Light, fruity – yes, it is good.' Louis Gautier smiled widely as he turned to cock his head towards Alisa. 'Do you not find it so?'

'I am not really a connoisseur of wine,' Alisa apologized, noting the reverent way he had inspected it.

'Ah, but you will learn. Zachary will teach you what qualities we look for in our wines. Has he shown you around the vineyards yet, and the winery?' At Alisa's negative shake of her head, Louis looked reprovingly at Zachary. 'The harvest season is almost upon us. Soon you will not have time to take her around.'

'When Alisa and I have been together, our thoughts have not been on grapes,' Zachary smiled wickedly across the table at Alisa.

'The mind of our new *vigneron* has been dwelling on his golden-haired wife and not on his golden-green grapes,' Louis laughed. 'That is what these lazy summer nights are for, while our succulent grapes grow heavy on their vines, huh, Momma?' Passing his plate to be served the dishes, Louis turned to Alisa and sighed. 'It will be good for you to learn about the grapes and the wines so you will know what it is that your husband is doing all the time. You should learn the history and tradition that abounds in our valley. My papa came here in 1896 with his papa all the way by ship from Bordeaux. They brought with them cuttings from the finest vines to marry with the American vines. The soil was good and the weather was good, but still they had to protect their vines from mildew, black rot and disease. Their wines were good. Yet when I was twenty-five they sent me off to France for five years that I could learn at my cousin's winery and become a good *vigneron*. It was there I met Momma.' He gazed fondly at his wife, who peered at him with a pleased yet shy look from behind her dark lashes. 'My papa and grandpapa have long been gone from us, but still we grow the grapes. From forty acres, we now own over five hundred acres. I would have bought this vineyard, too, but I am growing too old, and my daughter has not provided me with a son-in-law.'

'Papa, now that Zachary has been stolen away from me, who is left?' Renée laughed enchantingly at her father while eyeing Zachary with mock remorse. Alisa's teeth clamped tightly together as she met her husband's penetrating gaze.

'I have often wished that Zachary were my son,' Louis nodded. 'But it is not so. He is going to have a splendid vineyard one day. In a few years he will not have to sell any of his grapes to other wineries, for he will be bottling them all himself.'

'There will be few sold this year,' Zachary told them. 'I have purchased more cooperage, which arrived last week.'

'What kind?' Louis's eyes lit up with an anticipating glow.

'Stainless steel,' Zachary replied.

'After dinner you must take me to see them,' Louis ordered, lifting his glass towards his host before bringing it to his mouth.

Zachary returned his smile before his gaze slid to Alisa's knowing look. At last she knew where he had spent the money she had given him. She had had such a niggling doubt about it ever since she arrived at his home and discovered his large two-storey brick house so tastefully furnished. His dark eyes danced with mockery at her nearly evident relief. To avoid him Alisa turned to Mrs. Gautier and struggled to carry on a conversation with the gentle, quiet woman.

The men paused politely with the women at the end of the meal. Michael cornered Alisa for a moment, tossing in a few jibes about the ruby that 'her' money had bought.

'You're really trying to make this marriage look real,' he jeered. 'I don't think that ring is going to hold back Renée. She's a hot little tamale and she wants Zachary.'

'Michael, you know this never was a love match,' Alisa reminded him, her irritation growing.

'Still, you didn't seem too happy about the way they carried on at the table,' he pointed out.

'Neither did you,' she retorted, trying to keep her voice low so the rest of the guests couldn't hear. 'Is the competition too stiff?'

'Maybe, cousin dear, maybe.' Michael lifted his glass of wine before sauntering off in Renée's direction.

The men exchanged a few more pleasantries with the women before Zachary led the way towards the winery to show his new purchases to Louis. Once they had gone the conversation was controlled by Mrs. Stuart and Renée. Alisa sat quietly on the couch beside Mrs. Gautier wondering how she could tolerate being so obviously left out of the conversation. But Mrs. Gautier's attention was on her daughter as if she marvelled that anything so vivacious and volatile could have come from her. Alisa wondered, too.

She found her eyes wandering to the clock, wishing the time would pass more swiftly so that this tedious afternoon would come to an end. Alisa even caught herself wishing that Zachary would return from the winery so that his vitality would fill the room and stamp out the presence of these two boring women. But the pendulum of the mantel clock swung slowly and the ticking tempo couldn't drown out their voices. When she discovered her fingernails were making marks in the palm of her hand, Alisa decided she had had enough. With the excuse that she wanted to freshen up, she left the room.

Upstairs in the seclusion of her room, her pose of cool sophistication fell away. She glared into the mirror, suddenly angry at Zachary for ever having the dinner in the first place. He must have known what kind of woman his mother was. And springing Renée on her without any warning had been a choking humiliation. Alisa stared at the bottle of Chanel Number 5 on her dressing-table. She picked it up, carried it into the bathroom, and poured it down the sink. That was the fragrance that Renée had been wearing. Alisa discovered she hated it! A short, hollow laugh escaped her lips as she realized that the perfume was probably the most expensive drain freshener that had ever been used.

Re-entering her bedroom, Alisa wondered how long she could stay up here before her absence would be considered a breach of etiquette for a hostess. If it wouldn't be conceding victory to Mrs. Stuart and Renée, she wouldn't bother returning. Her pride wouldn't allow her to acknowledge defeat. She reapplied her lipstick, remembering how Michael had referred to it as putting on warpaint. In this case that was exactly what it was.

'Oh, this is where you are,' Renée drawled from the doorway, poised in its frame like a model making an entrance, before swishing into the room. 'I decided I'd better do some freshening up before the men returned.'

Alisa hid her surprise quickly, smiling coolly in welcoming Renée into her private room. 'I doubt whether the men, being what they are, will even notice that we've done anything,' she murmured, watching Renée fussing with her hair in front of the mirror.

'Zachary will notice. He always does, you know.' There was an intimacy in her reply that threatened to curl the hair on the back of Alisa's neck.

'Really? But then I'm sure you could tell me about a lot of Zachary's little foibles,' said Alisa, hoping her shaft of cold sarcasm had found its mark.

'Yes, I could.' The light of battle was in Renée's eyes as she turned to face Alisa. 'Zach and I have been close, very close, for a long time. As he has often said, we're two of a kind.'

'Perhaps that's why he tired of you,' Alisa retorted sharply.

Renée's face paled slightly before it was flooded with colour. 'Is this your room?' With deadly calm, she changed the subject, or so Alisa thought when she replied that it was. 'That's strange. I expected you to be in the master bedroom next door to where Zach sleeps. Why do you have separate rooms? Has he tired of you?'

'I can answer that one,' a bright voice rang out from the door.

'Christine!' Alisa exclaimed. 'What are you doing here?'

'I thought I'd find out how the party was going and the dark-haired lady in the blue dress said you were up here.' After answering Alisa's question, the child turned towards Renée. 'I know why they don't sleep in the same room.'

'Chris, you shouldn't be talking about such things,' Alisa interrupted quickly.

'Let the child talk,' Renée smiled. 'This should be very interesting.'

'I asked Zach one morning why you two didn't sleep together like Mommy and Daddy did.' Chris's voice rang with authority before a smile tugged at the corners of her mouth. 'You know what he told me? He said that Alisa snores so loud that he can't sleep!'

Alisa met the triumphant glance from the dark-haired girl as she grasped Christine by the shoulders to usher her out of the room.

'Can I sleep with you sometime, Lisa, so I can hear you snore?' Chris asked plaintively.

'No. Now run along outside and play,' Alisa ordered sharply.

'It seems I'm not the only one who's commented on your sleeping arrangements,' Renée laughed. 'They're hardly what one would expect from a newly married couple.'

'This is a personal matter between Zachary and myself.' Alisa turned away, unable to combat the frontal attack.

'Do you expect to be able to hold him by keeping him at arm's length?' Renée jeered. 'That may have been the way you got him to marry you, but, honey, you'd better come across with the goods or you're going to lose him.'

'And you'll be right there to catch him, won't you?' Alisa reached for her cigarettes, hoping her hand wouldn't tremble and reveal how thoroughly Renée's jibes were getting through.

'You bet I will! He's a virile, passionate man and I know how to satisfy him.' The long dark locks were tossed over her shoulder in a positive gesture. 'You noticed the way he looked at me today. You can bet he's got a lot to remember about what went on between us. I intend that he'll have a lot more.'

'Isn't it dangerous, giving away your plans like this

to the enemy?' Alisa queried coldly.

'Not with you it isn't.' Smug sarcasm rang harshly in Renée's voice. 'You're a very lovely but cold work of art. You may have the equipment to keep him, but you don't know how to use it.'

'I may not know how to swing my hips provocatively and sway them in front of a man, or how to simper and pander to his ego. But I will not tolerate you mooning over him in my presence, making eyes or whatever you call it. If you think for one minute that I'm going to let you throw yourself all over my husband without doing a thing about it, you're wrong!' Her voice shook with enraged anger as Alisa faced Renée. 'There will be no more secret meetings or intimate chats on the telephone. Never again will I allow you into this house to—'

'Alisa!' Zachary's harsh commanding voice broke behind her.

Almost unwillingly, she turned to him, the sharp edge of her anger dulling slightly upon meeting the shimmering brilliance of his. The fiery black eyes held hers for an eternity of a second before they moved to Renée. There was a shade of softness in his gaze as it rested on her. Alisa glanced back and was stunned to see two small tears trickling down Renée's cheeks. With a raised eyebrow, Alisa realized that she had underestimated Renée's ability as an actress.

'Would you excuse us, Renée?' Zachary asked with deadly quietness.

'I'm sorry, Zach. I never dreamed this would happen,' she whispered in return.

Alisa's anger once again rose to its former peak as she

watched Renée leave the room, knowing that little speech was for Zachary's benefit and he had fallen for it completely. As the door closed behind the tangerine silk dress, Alisa drew herself up arrogantly to face him.

'You have a headache, Alisa.'

The strange statement momentarily stunned her with its tightly-controlled tone. 'What are you talking about?'

'I said you aren't feeling well, so you'd better stay in your room,' he repeated, his voice raising slightly in emphasis.

'You're partially right.' Her brilliant blue eyes clashed fiercely with his. 'I am sick! Sick of bowing to your mother's offensive comments, of hearing what a more perfect couple you and Renée would make, of answering Renée's questions about our sleeping habits! I'm sick, sick of it all!' She fairly screamed the last.

'I can understand how my mother can grate on you,' he allowed. 'But you had no business inviting Renée up here to your room. Whatever she said you brought it on yourself.' There was no relenting in the fire of his gaze.

'I didn't invite her up here!' Alisa corrected him. 'She charged up here on her own. The way she acts you'd think she was the mistress of this house as well as the mistress of its owner!'

'I will not have you talking about Renée in that manner!'

'You will not! My, how chivalrous of you,' sarcastically. 'You defend your mistress and not your wife. What about me? Look how you just humiliated me in

116

front of her! Am I to stand idly by while you ask Renée to leave the room so you can reprimand me in private for speaking the truth?'

'I thought that today at least you could be civil towards my guests. The Gautiers have been my friends for years and I expected you to treat the entire family with respect.'

'And how was Renée supposed to treat me – or isn't there any standards that mistresses are supposed to follow?' Alisa jeered.

His jaw clenched tightly together. At the side of his face, a muscle twitched to reveal the depth of his anger. 'I want you to stay here in this room while I go down to explain to our guests that you're indisposed.'

'I will not stay here and admit victory to that little tramp!' Alisa denied vehemently.

In one stride, she was imprisoned in his arms, his face glaring darkly inches from hers. 'And I will not tolerate your insolence. You demand the respect of a wife, yet you're not willing to carry out the duties of a wife. But we can change that.'

He crushed her to his chest, imprisoning her arms between their two bodies as his lips covered hers. Wildly she struggled to be free of his touch, but his hand clasped her hair and twisted her into stillness. The pressure of his kiss increased until her lips were ground against her teeth. Still mercilessly, it went on. At last, when she thought her very breath would be denied her, Zachary released her. Her hand went to her bruised and battered lips, attempting to wipe away the degradation and humiliation of his touch.

'You stay here,' he muttered hoarsely, wiping the

lipstick from his mouth with a handkerchief, 'or I'll introduce you to more wifely duties!'

Alisa found her hand closing around the empty perfume bottle on the dressing-table. In the next instant, she had hurled it at the closing door, taking vicarious pleasure out of the explosive sound of its contact with the wood.

CHAPTER FIVE

'ARE you ready, Chris?' Alisa picked up a pair of white lace gloves, then discarded them since they couldn't go over her ring.

There was a flash of white-shoed feet accompanied by a whirling strawberry-coloured skirt as Chris danced into the room in excitement. 'I'm ready!' she cried shrilly. 'Oh, hurry, Lisa!'

'You're not starting to school yet,' Alisa laughed. 'We're only registering you today so that you can go.'

But her hand was quickly taken by a smaller one that insistently led her out of the bedroom towards the staircase. At the base of the stairs Zachary stood silently watching their approach. Alisa stared at him, the surprise at seeing him at this time of day registering on her face.

'Zach, are you ready, too?' Christine released Alisa's hand and raced down the steps ahead of her.

'Are you going with us?' Alisa asked, reaching the bottom step and gazing into his inscrutable face with a combination of distrust and disbelief.

'We're going as a family today,' Chris announced, now taking Zachary's hand and tugging towards the door. 'Is everything ready?'

His pace was too slow for her, so Chris dashed ahead, out the door towards the waiting car. Alisa glanced puzzledly at him.

'Is what ready?' she asked.

'After the registration is over, we're going on a picnic,' he said calmly, his gaze never once straying to see Alisa's reaction. 'Harvesting will begin next week when school starts. As Christine pointed out to me, this will be the only time we can do anything as a family.'

'How unfortunate that you ever promised her we would,' Alisa said grimly.'

'I don't mind. She's an exhilarating, uninhibited person, luckily not marred by the pessimism of her sister,' Zachary jeered. 'After all you've sacrificed for her already, surely an afternoon in my company can be tolerated.'

She glared at him coldly. If only she could be sure this afternoon was for the benefit of Christine. There was no doubt in her mind that Chris had initiated the idea, but the question was why had Zachary consented to it after ignoring Alisa's existence since the disastrous dinner party.

They had reached the car when his questioning 'Well?' demanded a response. She sighed heavily.

'You've left everything until the last minute, so I hardly have any choice in the matter, do I?' she retorted sharply.

'Does that irritate you?' Zachary opened the car door for her.

'Yes, it does,' she hissed so that Christine who was already in the back seat of the wagon wouldn't hear.

Zachary smiled down at her as he closed the door for her, a wickedly smug expression that brought her teeth together. Before sliding into the driver's seat, Zachary removed his cream tan sports jacket and laid it on the back of the seat. The late August sun beat warmly into the windows of the car so that the tan print short-sleeved shirt was more than sufficient attire for him. Christine bobbed happily behind them as the car pulled out on the lane. Her chattering, interspersed with comments from either Alisa or Zachary depending on whom she was directing her conversation to, dotted the journey into St. Helena. Arriving at the school, she skipped ahead of them to the entrance.

'I believe we're both adult enough to lay aside our personal feelings,' Zachary said in a low voice, 'and make this an enjoyable afternoon for Christine's sake.'

'I'm very willing to do it for her,' Alisa replied. 'As long as you can contain your jeering, I would hardly have cause to retaliate.'

'Then it's a truce.' Zachary held the school door open for her with an amiable smile. 'We may even surprise ourselves and find the afternoon pleasant even to each other.'

Alisa's dubious glance spoke clearly that she doubted such a thing could happen, but she didn't reply.

The transferring of Christine's records from her previous school, the enrolment in the third grade and the subsequent paper work that that entailed was quickly completed and the three were back in the car driving north of town. Their short journey took them past several vineyards welcoming visitors to tour their facilities before Zachary turned the car into a small park. Christine bounded out of the car almost the minute it came to a halt, racing over towards an old wooden structure that dominated the grounds.

'It's called the Old Bale Mill,' Zachary explained as he and Alisa joined the darting child. 'It was built by a Dr. Edward Bale to grind grain for early Napa Valley pioneers. They're recently rebuilt it from its almost ruined state so that now it looks almost workable, although it's never been tried.'

Alisa walked over the jagged stones to stand beside the huge undershot waterwheel that had once been the power that had driven the grinding stones. The branches of a nearby tree rested against the towering wooden wheel, empasizing its lack of use.

'It's really quite impressive, isn't it?' Alisa commented as Zachary joined her, his tie removed and thrown over his shoulder and the top two buttons of his shirt unbuttoned.

'A necessity in its day,' he agreed.

I'm going to find us a place to have our picnic,' Chris called before scampering away to investigate the rest of the park.

By mutual consent the pair made their way across the stones, Zachary leading the way a half step ahead of Alisa. Her white sandals had a small but slender heel, hardly made for negotiating the tricky rocks. As she stepped off the flat surface on to another, the first rock slipped, sending Alisa rocketing forward. Two tanned arms reached forward, and her fall was arrested by Zachary's broad chest.

'Are you all right?' His hands were firmly around her waist, supporting her shaky legs.

'Yes,' she gulped. Her own hands were gripping his forearms tightly to retain her upright position. Beneath her fingers she could feel the erratic race of his pulse. 'I think your heart is beating as fast as mine,' Alisa said with a weak, jesting laugh.

'Probably at the surprise of finding you clinging so tenaciously to me.' Her gaze flew up to his face at the amused yet completely serious tone of Zachary's voice. The ardent fire in his dark eyes mesmerized her. 'Do you know, when you put aside that mask of cold reserve, you're a very beautiful and desirable woman?'

Her fingers immediately relaxed their hold on his arm.

'And you,' her voice was husky and soft, with the barest tremble in it, 'can show surprising concern when it suits you.'

The soft curve of his lips broadened into a wide smile that emitted a quiet chuckle. 'I think you just put me down,' he said, releasing his own hold on her until only a hand rested lightly against her side. 'Which means we'd better catch up with Christine.'

This time they walked side by side, Alisa knowing no way to shake off his hand without arousing his mockery. The day was too peaceful and the park was too serene to let it be disturbed by their bickering. Besides there was Chris to be considered.

'I do admire the way you've insisted on having Christine,' Zachary said. 'I don't think of any other woman with the looks and wealth that you have who would have done what you have, especially for a half-sister who's so much younger than you. Have you considered exactly what the future will be like for you?'

'Are you trying to tell me what a liability she is?' Alisa smiled. 'I'm not really making any great sacrifice.

It can't really be considered a sacrifice when you're doing it for someone you love.' She glanced up at him, expecting to see the mockery and cynicism on his face, only to find him regarding her with serious interest. 'It's a terrible cliché, I know, but I want her to grow up differently from the way I did. I want her to know a sense of security, that I'll always be there if she needs me because I love her.'

'And your childhood, what was it like?'

'One long string of Mother's male admirers and husbands. I think the day she died she couldn't have even told you what my father's name was,' Alisa laughed, trying to be funny, but a bit of the bitterness peeped through.

'I assumed it was something like that,' Zachary nodded. 'That's the reason for your dislike of the male sex.'

'No, I think it has more to do with my disbelief that love between the sexes really exists. I believe the magnet drawing the two together is the animal desire for sexual satisfaction.'

'Which is the reason your magnet has been switched to the neutral position – right?' Zachary gazed down at her with quizzical thoughtfulness. 'There is love, Alisa. I hope someday you'll discover it for yourself.'

'You're speaking as if you know it for a fact,' she replied after a short pause over the soft earnestness of his statement.

'Do you find it hard to believe there's such a thing as love, or that *I* could be in love?' Zachary teased.

Alisa stared up at him, her head tilted, trying to discover why he seemed so peculiarly different. His hair was just as ebony black as his eyes beneath their lazily curling black lashes. Her eyes reverted to looking at the ground in front of them.

'I don't find it hard to believe that you want Renée. I'm sure you find her a very beautiful woman.'

'There you go again,' Zachary laughed, 'inserting "want" for love.'

'It's practically the same thing.'

'When you need someone because you love them, that's love. You're talking about the reverse when you love someone because you need them. They're two very different things, Alisa.' He was staring off ahead of them when she looked up to see if she could read the expression on his face. The only thing she was able to determine was that he truly believed what he was saying. Feeling her gaze studying him, Zachary turned to meet it with the corner of his mouth lifting in a sympathetic smile. 'I can see you don't quite believe me. And that questioning gleam in your blue eyes tells me that you're about to argue the point, so let's change the subject. This afternoon is for Christine, and you and I are supposed to be observing a truce.'

Reluctantly Alisa agreed. But she found her thoughts reverting back to the subject with uncomfortable repetitiveness. Not even the exuberant Christine could completely pull her out of her contemplation as she gave in readily to her younger sister's demands that the picnic be held on the grass and not on the tables provided for such purposes. The hamper from the car was filled with food — cold roast chicken garnished with carrot sticks, cherry tomatoes, and celery sticks were in one box. In another there were buttered slices of egg twist bread. For dessert, there were fresh pears and Port Salut cheese. As Alisa spread the food out on the checked cloth, Zachary produced wine glasses and a bottle of wine.

'Unfortunately this is not a bottle of my wine,' he said as he uncorked it, pouring the ruby red liquid into the two glasses. 'It's Cabernet Sauvignon from the Gautier winery. I promise you it's the very best of the California red wines.'

'Can I have some grape juice, too, Zachary?' Christine piped from where she knelt beside him.

'You aren't old enough to drink wine,' Alisa smiled.

'Let her have a taste. She might as well know what it is that her new brother does. She's been at the winery often enough, she deserves to have a taste,' declared Zachary, holding out his own glass for Chris to sip.

The red liquid had barely touched her lips when Chrstine pulled away, her mouth curling in the supreme expression of distaste. 'It's rotten!' she exclaimed, staring at Zachary as if he had attempted to poison her. 'It doesn't taste like grape juice at all!'

'No, Peanut, wine is made from grapes. Their aroma is there, but it doesn't taste like grape juice,' Zachary laughed heartily.

'How can you drink that stuff?' The small shoulders shuddered.

This time it was Alisa who laughed. 'You grow accustomed to it, Chris.'

'Not me, I never will!'

'Nora must have known that little girls don't care too much for wine,' Zachary reached into a second hamper and took out a thermos bottle, 'because she also sent along some lemonade, if I'm not mistaken.'

'Oh, goody!' Chris's sudden burst of elation halted as she turned her head to Zachary. 'Do you suppose Nora will pack my lunch for me for school, so I can take it with me on the bus like the rest of the kids?'

'I think most of the children eat their lunch at the school,' said Zachary, 'but I'm sure if you want her to she'll arrange something with Mrs. March.'

'I don't think Chris needs to ride on the bus.' Alisa's head shook slowly back and forth as she spoke. 'I can very easily drive her to school in the morning and pick her up in the afternoon.'

'No, Alisa, I want to ride on the school bus,' Chris protested with a wail. 'I don't want to be different from the other kids. I want to ride like they do.'

'That's a point to be well taken, Alisa,' Zachary glanced at her briefly over the rim of his wine glass.

'Yes . . .' Still Alisa hesitated, her gaze on the pleading eyes that were staring earnestly back at her, the small lips forming the word 'Please'. 'If that's the way you want it, Chris, you can ride in the school bus like the rest of the children.'

Later, after everyone had eaten their fill and Chris had raced off to examine the Bale Mill more closely, Alisa and Zachary remained. Alisa had finished packing away the remnants of their meal while Zachary had stretched himself out on his side in the grass.

'I'm glad you agreed to let Chris ride on the bus,' he said, as Alisa curled her legs to one side and straightened her skirt. 'I think it will make her adjustment to her new school and her new friends that much easier.'

127

'I hope so,' Alisa murmured, gazing after the bright copper hair that was visible in the distance. 'I hope she doesn't become too attached to her new friends, or it will be hard on her to leave at the end of the school year.'

'She wouldn't have to leave.' Zachary withdrew his cigarette case, lifted it towards Alisa, who nodded that she would like one.

'What do you mean, she wouldn't have to leave? You know at the end of the school year we'll be getting a divorce and I'll be leaving.' Beneath the pale golden hair, her forehead was creased with a frown.

'You'll be leaving my house, yes, but that doesn't mean you have to leave the district, does it? I should think that if Christine were happy here, you would stay.' The gold lighter flicked its fire to the tips of the cigarettes now between Zachary's lips.

As he passed the lit cigarette to Alisa, she knew with startling clarity that once they were divorced she would never stay in the same area that Zachary was in. Nodding that it was always possible that she could stay, she placed the cigarette between her lips, the warmth of his still on the filter. Her mind recalled the previous touch of his lips, harsh and cruel, shaming her and denouncing her piteous attempt to resist him. The memory was as clear as if he had left a brand. And in that instant, their truce was dissolved. Zachary must have sensed it, too, for he almost immediately rose and began packing the things away into the station wagon. The serene peacefulness of the afternoon was gone.

CHAPTER SIX

THE first weeks of September inched by, each day seeming to pass slower than the last. The flurry of activity in the mornings as Christine would race to meet her school bus was accented by the hours that stretched ahead for Alisa to fill until the bus brought Christine home that afternoon. The grape harvest had begun. The vineyards were a hum of people and vehicles, picking and transporting the grapes to the winery on the hill above the house. And Zachary was directing the activity, rising and going to the fields long before the workers arrived and staying at the winery long after they had left. Alisa and Christine had usually had their evening meal long before he even arrived to dine. Very occasionally Zachary would join Alisa in the living-room, there sitting in companionable silence before excusing himself to pore over his paper work in the den.

During the first empty days, Alisa had wandered aimlessly around the house and yard, noting the changing autumn colours of the grapevines from green to brown-gold, and the ivy on the house slowly turning its flame red. Her walks often led her in the direction of the winery, but she always halted her steps in the shadow of the oak trees and gazed absently at the traffic shifting back and forth between the buildings and the vineyard. Zachary took his noon meals in those buildings. The returning half-eaten sandwiches were evidence that his attention was on his grapes.

Several times Alisa had heard the sound of hoofbeats on the gravelled road. She knew of only one person who rode a horse and that was Renée, although Zachary never made any mention of her presence. It was extremely unlikely that he would, knowing her feelings about Renée. Still it angered Alisa that Zachary was still meeting her, openly defying Alisa.

The combination of inactivity and unwillingness to meet Renée accidentally on one of her walks had driven Alisa back to the house. There she prevailed upon the housekeeper to let her help in taking care of the house, insisting that Nora had plenty to do supervising the kitchen, the laundry, the shopping and her own home without doing all the cleaning herself. So, slowly, over a period of days, Alisa took on the daily tasks herself, making beds, dusting furniture and floors, and anything else that would speed the passing of the hours.

Alisa opened the door to the master bedroom where Zachary slept and stepped inside, carrying one of his suits just back from the dry-cleaners. Her eyes trailed appreciatively around the room, admiring the ivory-coloured walls and the red velvet of the curtains. Straightening, dusting, and making the bed in this room had become her custom. Since the first day that she had nervously entered the room and discovered its elegant Mediterranean furniture on the plush red carpet, she had fallen in love with the room. She had known a moment of envy that Zachary occupied the room until she remembered, with a shiver, that as his wife she could share it with him. She was content to admire it and care for it.

But her special love was the adjoining room. It was too small to be considered a bedroom and too large for a dressing-room. Dirty, pale cream walls spoke of its neglect, as did the two lonely pieces of furniture, a daybed and a wardrobe. Alisa had known immediately its purpose – a nursery. Even now, as she opened the door and entered the room, she could see it transformed in her mind's eyes. The walls would be papered in a gentle green and white stripe to suit either a boy or a girl and the windows and woodwork would be painted an enamel white. The curtains could be an airy dotted swiss if it were a girl, or a coarse, nubby linen if it were a boy. In the place of the daybed, there would be a shiny white crib with dancing butterflies hanging down from a string. Near the window would be a rocking chair and a small floor lamp. In Alisa's imagination, the setting was very clear.

She stood in the centre of the room, unconsciously hugging the suit against her pastel coral sundress. As her head bent, the material brushed her cheek and she pulled away with a jerk. A tiny smile of embarrassment lifted the corners of her mouth at the wanderings of her thoughts. Alisa brushed the jacket sleeve against her cheek again, wondering curiously how many wives caressed their husbands' clothes like sentimental idiots and dreamed of the babies they would have. She turned with a cynically amused smile, telling herself how glad she was that she wasn't that kind of a woman.

'I wondered how long your daydream was going to last.' Zachary stood in the doorway, a hand braced against the door-jamb. 'You looked so content that I hated to disturb you.'

'What are you doing here? You're supposed to be at the vineyards.' Her face coloured slightly at his questioning look.

'I have to go into town to pick up a spare part, so I decided to shower and change first,' he explained, still not moving from the door even though Alisa stood expectantly waiting for him to move. 'A better question is what are you doing here?'

'I was just going to put your suit away. Nora picked it up from the cleaners this morning.' Alisa hated the defensive weakness in her voice.

'My closet is in this room.' His head turned slightly to indicate the room behind him.

'I know. I've been in there several times before.'

'Have you?' The eyebrows over Zachary's left eye arched in mockery.

'I usually straighten things up a bit,' Alisa added, not liking the gleam that was shining in his dark eyes.

'If you don't stop crushing that coat, we're going to have to send it back to the cleaners to be pressed.' His glance slid from the two slightly bright spots on her cheek to her hands that were digging into the suit.

Alisa nearly dropped it in her hurry to release her damaging hold. 'If you would move out of the way, I'd hang it up,' she managed to say huffily.

'By all means.' Zachary shifted his position to lean against one side of the door, permitting her enough room to pass through.

She glanced at him hesitantly, wishing he would

have moved out of the doorway altogether. It would do her no good to let him see he riled her, so assuming as much coolness as possible, Alisa left the safety of the centre of the nursery to walk to the door. As she was about to slip past him, his arm moved out to bar the way.

'Would you please let me through?' She eyed him frostily.

His other arm moved to the opposite side preventing her from retreating into the nursery. Zachary moved away from the opposite door-jamb to stand closer.

'What were you thinking about a minute ago when you were standing there dreaming in the middle of the room?' he asked, watching her with that lazy regard that hid the fiery brightness of his eyes.

'If you must know, I was visualizing what it would look like if it were redecorated.' A trace of exasperation and frustration sharpened her words.

'Do you know that it was built as a nursery?'

'I assumed it was,' she replied with cold arrogance. 'Now, will you let me through?'

'I noticed you called Nora, Nora. You two are finally getting along. What brought about this change?' Zachary ignored her request again.

'There didn't seem any point in insisting on formality when everyone else in this house doesn't.' Alisa glared at him, angered by his relentless refusal to let her pass. 'I've had a great deal of time on my hands since Chris has started school, so I decided to help Nora around the house. It's as simple as that.'

'You've probably been at a loose end, haven't you? In another few weeks, the harvesting will be over and

I'll have a bit more free time.'

'That should please Renée,' Alisa said sarcastically.

'I think it must have been your perfume that's lulled me to sleep these past nights.' Zachary moved closer still, shrugging off her barbed words. 'It's a nice perfume, full of the innocent essence of spring flowers.' His head bent slowly towards her as she stiffened and held herself rigidly erect. Alisa could feel the feathery lightness of his lips as he touched the side of her neck. 'Where do you put it? Here, on the side of your neck.' Zachary continued his nuzzling quest. 'In the hollow of your shoulder.' His lips gently followed the trail of his words while Alisa stood motionless, determined to let him see how little his lovemaking affected her. But it was a strange and sensuous sensation that covered her arms with goosebumps.

'Did your daydreaming include populating the nursery?' The unexpectedness of his question pulled her sharply out of her reverie of his actions, although the persistent nibbling on her neck didn't cease.

'Of course not!' Alisa breathed out in a shocked whisper.

'That's a pity. I suppose you've noticed my bed is very large.' Zachary moved away long enough to gaze deeply into her blue eyes before his lips resumed their wandering on the opposite side of her neck.

'What's the matter? Haven't you seen Renée for a few days?' Alisa questioned indignantly.

'As a matter of fact; I saw her this morning.' Alisa could hear the amusement in his voice. 'But that doesn't solve your problem of a baby. What do you suppose our baby would be like?'

Alisa was beginning to feel overpowered by his near-ness. His blue shirt was completely unbuttoned. Her hands, even if she wanted to resist, couldn't push him away without touching the nakedness of his chest. The fragrance of his cologne with its masculine earthiness grew stronger with each breath she took. But it was the persistent caress of his mouth against the sensitive skin of her neck that was creating the most unrest inside her. She realized that she was trying to ward off a master in the art of making love.

'I'm not a maid who's forced to let her lord indulge his whims, Zachary,' she said sharply. 'And I assure you I've never even considered a ... a ... baby, and least of all yours!'

'Why don't you consider it now?' Zachary tilted his head back and smiled down at her wickedly before he moved forward again, this time to claim her lips in a gentle but ardent kiss.

Determinedly Alisa kept her lips cool and unre-sponsive to his touch, despite the increasing fire that threatened to melt her icy reserve. When she thought she couldn't make it any longer, Zachary moved away.

'Does it give you a sense of power to know you can arouse me?' he asked.

Alisa studied him carefully. Except for the burning fire in his gaze, there didn't seem to be any other thing that supported his statement that she had aroused him. He even seemed to be laughing at her.

'Did you feel any sense of defeat when you failed to arouse me?' she returned sharply.

'Oh, but I did arouse you,' Zachary smiled. 'Your heart was racing faster than a thoroughbred horse. Too bad I have to go into town, or our little diversion could have lasted longer. It would be interesting to see how long you could resist returning my kiss.'

'You're the most arrogant, and vain—' Alisa began, angered uncontrollably by his assumption that she would have wanted to kiss him.

'The word is man,' Zachary supplied, a confidently knowing smile curling the corners of his mouth.

Alisa didn't spare the time thinking about what she was doing. Her hand raced faster than her thoughts that commanded it. Only after the sting of the contact with his cheek registered did she realize that she had slapped him. Zachary looked at her. Then with the most irritating composure, he laughed.

'You'd better hurry up and get out of here,' he chuckled still. 'Hang up my suit or whatever you were going to do. I want to shower and change my clothes. You're welcome to stay if you want to.'

Alisa wished there wasn't any carpet on the floor so that the sound of her stamping feet could echo in his ears. But unfortunately that wasn't the case. With an efficiency of movement, she had the suit hung up and was slamming the door as, from the corner of her eye, she saw the blue shirt go sailing across the room to land on the velvet bedspread.

CHAPTER SEVEN

'I wish you'd leave those windows for one of the men to get, Mrs. Stuart,' Nora called from her vantage point at the base of the ladder. 'It's much too dangerous for you to be climbing around up there like that. Zachary would have my hide if he knew!'

'These windows were so dirty from all that dust flying around from the trucks that you couldn't see out of them,' Alisa didn't pause as one hand clutched the ladder tightly while the other reached over to wipe a windowpane dry. 'Besides, this is the last one and I'm all done.'

'All I can say is thank goodness it's the end of October and the last field will be picked tomorrow,' the housekeeper replied, firmly holding the ladder while Alisa started down from her second storey perch.

Alisa wasn't too sure she agreed. The harvesting had kept Zachary tied down and prevented any more chance meetings that might have led to further scenes such as the one in his bedroom. Although she had grown quite fond of Nora, Alisa could hardly confide a reluctance to the end of the harvest season. Instead she said that she would welcome the peace and quiet after the endless hum of activity.

'I just came out to make sure there was nothing else you'd be needing me for this afternoon and to tell you that your lunch was all ready whenever you get cleaned up,' Nora stated.

'There's not a thing,' Alisa assured her, reaching the bottom rung of the ladder. 'You go on to town and visit your grandson and don't give a thought to anything out here.'

'He's only in the hospital with a tonsillectomy. He'll be home tomorrow. But you know how children are. He expects his grandma to see him.'

'He's in Chris's class at school, so you can tell him for her to get better in a hurry. According to her they have a really spooky party planned for Hallowe'en,' Alisa laughed, wiping her hands on her faded denims.

'If you won't be needing anything, I'll be going,' Nora repeated after promising she would relay Chris's message.

'There's nothing,' Alisa assured her again.

It took several more minutes of conversation before Nora was confident that she was leaving the house in capable hands and there would be no unforeseen calamities while she was gone. At last she was away, honking the horn at Alisa as she drove out the lane. Sighing heavily, Alisa gathered her various rags and bucket, and trudged into the house. She hesitated inside, debating whether to shower and change before eating her lunch or just wash for the time being. She decided on the latter, as the gnawing pangs of hunger increased their cry.

As she neared the kitchen, Alisa could hear the mumbled grumblings of Mrs. March, the cook. Cupboard doors slammed loudly, combined with the clanging of utensils. Grimacing to herself, Alisa squared her shoulders to face the short-tempered woman.

'Hello, Mrs. March,' she said cheerily as she swung through the door. 'How are things this morning?'

'Terrible, if you must know,' the woman snarled. Her brown hair, laced with premature grey, was drawn tightly against her skull to gather in a bun at the back of her head. 'I ain't one to complain, you know that.'

'Not much,' Alisa thought to herself, before banishing such thoughts with the remembrance of what an excellent cook she was.

'But that woman,' obviously meaning Nora, 'goes off and leaves me when she knows I'm in the middle of making a *torte* for dessert tonight. Why, it'll take me an hour or more before it's done!' Another cupboard door slammed shut.

'I don't understand. What's the problem?' Alisa asked, trying to assume a pose that would quiet the barely controlled tantrum.

'Would you tell me how I'm going to do this *torte* and still get Mr. Stuart's lunch out to him by one?' Her voice rang shrilly through the kitchen.

'Why didn't you ask her to take it out to him before she left?' Alisa asked, a sinking feeling descending upon her stomach.

'And have her start raving on about her grandson again? Not on your life!' Mrs. March shook her head firmly. 'I guess I just might as well forget all about this *torte*. Throw it in the garbage. Nobody in this house cares about all the time and trouble I take trying to make their food to put on the table. They just go on about their business without so much as a by your leave!'

'You know how much Mr. Stuart and I appreciate

your efforts,' Alisa soothed in vain.

'Well, there's some in this house, not mentioning any names, who just don't care one way or another.'

'I'm sure there's a solution to this.' She knew what the solution was, but Alisa dreaded taking it.

'And just what would that be? Calling Mr. Stuart and telling him to come down here to eat his lunch, with him working as hard as he does! Why, he'd just skip eating altogether.' A spoon clattered loudly into a bowl.

'It's simpler than that, Mrs. March,' Alisa smiled. 'I'll just take his lunch up to him after I've finished with mine.'

'Now why didn't I think of that myself?' The dull hazel eyes turned on her with the barest hint of gratitude in their depths.

'I imagine you were just too busy,' Alisa said, a cajoling smile on her face while her heart sank to her feet at the propsect of going to the winery with Zachary's lunch. 'No, I'll just wash up and have my own lunch.'

'I'll have everything fixed all up for you in the morning-room, Mrs. Stuart. You're a real life-saver,' Mrs. March nodded firmly.

Alisa's thoughts were more like this was a grand way to ruin what started out to be a beautiful day. But there was no other course of action open. She sighed, pushing her hands under the fast-running water from the tap and scrubbing at them briskly. There was always the possibility that Zachary would be occupied elsewhere and she could just leave the lunch for him. It was a small hope to cling to, but it was the only one she had.

Her own meal, though attractively appetizing, didn't appeal to her taste buds – either that or the prospect of seeing Zachary had robbed her of her appetite. In any case, Alisa pushed her plate away with only half the food consumed. While her resolution to take up his lunch held, Alisa returned to the kitchen and picked up the covered tray of food that Mrs. March had prepared.

The heady bouquet of fermenting wine filled the air as she walked determinedly on the tree-lined path to the winery. Alisa had no idea at all where she could find Zachary or where his office was. Shortly after reaching the clearing, she realized that she didn't have to be concerned about it. She remained motionless for a moment in the shadow of the trees, staring at a Zachary completely shirtless, his torso gleaming with perspiration until he resembled a bronze statue. She tried to shake away the unnerving feeling, telling herself of the many men she'd seen dressed in much less at swimming pools and beaches. But Zachary seemed surrounded by an earthy virility that was disturbingly compelling.

Finally she forced her gaze to include the man at Zachary's side. With the barest acknowledgment of relief, Alisa recognized Paul, She felt sure Paul would preclude any forced intimacy that Zachary might have attempted. Armed now with fresh confidence to face her husband's all-encompassing vitality, Alisa walked forward with poised, sure strides.

'Well, well,' said Zachary, as he turned his head in her direction at the crunching of her canvas shoes on the gravelled road. 'Look who's finally entering the parlour of the spider.'

'Hello, Zachary, Paul,' Alisa said calmly, halting beside them. 'Nora went into town to see her grandson so I volunteered to bring your lunch.'

'Alisa,' Paul acknowledged with a wide smile and a nod. 'You're looking very well, as usual.'

'There seems to be a fresh glow on her cheeks,' Zachary's gaze danced over her face. 'Maybe it's just that I'm accustomed to seeing you so immaculately dressed that I've forgotten how enchanting you look with your hair flying every which way, like that morning in Las Vegas when we were married.'

'Trust him to remember that,' Alisa thought in irritation, but forbearing to say it aloud: 'I wish I'd known you were here. I could have had Mrs. March get you some lunch, too, Paul.'

'I had a very late breakfast.' His blue eyes glowed at her warmly.

'Where would you like me to—' The rest of Alisa's sentence was broken off by the sound of spinning tyres racing up the hill road. All three turned to watch the bright red sports car brake to a halt beside them in a swirling dust-blown haze. Alisa's lips compressed tightly as she recognized Renée behind the wheel. The convertible top was down, so instead of climbing out, Renée stood up and perched herself on top of the back seat.

'Isn't this convenient!' she exclaimed. Her dark eyes rolled admiringly from Zachary and Paul to burn brightly at Alisa. 'I came to let you know that Papa has set the date for our party. It will be a week from this Saturday. You all can consider it a formal invitation.'

'A party?' Alisa questioned.

'Papa always has a party to celebrate a successful harvest. It's very small and informal and loads of fun. Isn't that right, Zach?' She turned her full charming smile on him.

'It's a little windy with the top down, isn't it?' Zachary said with that enigmatical smile playing with the corners of his mouth.

'You know how I like the feel of the wind running through my hair. It reminds me of . . . well, you know what it reminds me of,'.Renée finished coyly.

'Where did you want me to put your lunch, Zachary?' Alisa asked sharply.

'Paul, show her where my office is,' he directed before turning back to Renée with an arm stretched out against the car to brace him. 'How was your harvest?'

With rigidly squared shoulders, Alisa accepted Paul's guiding hand. Zachary had dismissed her rather smoothly, she thought with glowering anger. Shooing her off so he could go ahead and play. Her throat tightened as she heard Renée's husky laugh trailing after her.

'Doesn't she know where your office is?' If Renée hadn't meant Alisa to hear that remark, she could have lowered her voice by several degrees. But Alisa knew she was meant to hear it so that the point could be driven home more sharply that she was the outsider and not Renée.

Paul·led her through a large double door, down a twisting corridor amid stacks of large barrels to a small hallway. There he opened a door into a large, but sparsely furnished office consisting of one desk and chair and a large table surrounded by stiff wooden chairs.

'This is Zachary's office which occasionally doubles as a tasting room,' Paul announced. 'You can put the tray on his desk. He'll be in shortly, I'm sure.'

Alisa wasn't that sure, but she put the tray down on the desk as he had directed. She glanced idly around the room, allowing her gaze to trail out the door to where the barrels they had just passed were still visible.

'What are those barrels for?' she asked.

'They're used for wine in various stages of ageing,' Paul replied, stepping with her to the doorway for a better view. 'All the casks you see are made out of French oak. Would you like me to show you around the winery?'

The making of wine always seemed so mysterious to Alisa that she agreed readily. Besides, she wasn't exactly eager to return outside where Renée and Zachary were evidently still in conference.

'Then I suggest we begin at the beginning with the grapes,' Paul smiled, pausing at the doorway for Alisa to precede him.

Again they went through the twisting corridor, only instead of ending up at the double door to the outside, somewhere they had taken a turn and were entering another building. They walked to the front of the building where grapes were being unloaded into a large machine.

'This is the stemmer/crusher, a Garolla type used by nearly all the California vineyards. It put the grapestompers out of business,' he added with a gleam lighting his twinkling blue eyes. 'The grapes are fed into the machine either by lugs or in this case, by hopper so that our large gondolas can be emptied all at once. Paddles revolve inside the cylinder, popping off the stems of the grape and breaking their skins at the same time. On the other side of the machine, the stems are blown out. Here we're working with white grapes,' he pointed to the green-gold globes of fruit that were tumbling into the machine. 'These will go from the crusher to a press where their juice is squeezed from them before fermentation begins.'

Paul had already led Alisa on to examine the press, nodding and dodging workmen as they worked their way on.

'Red grapes ferment first so that the desired colour and other characteristics of red wines can be extracted from their skins.' He was leading her on again to stand amidst a group of enormously tall tanks. 'Here's where the fermentation takes place. The redwood tanks on this side of the building are for red wines. As you can see, or perhaps you can't,' Paul laughed as Alisa attempted to stand on tiptoe and was several feet away from the top, 'the top of these tanks are open. But oxygen is a deadly enemy for white wines, so their fermenting tanks are closed.'

'What are those things at the base of the tanks?' Alisa asked.

'Those are cooling devices to control the temperature of the fermentation. Occasionally, you'll see men inserting a thermometer to make sure that the fermentation is not taking place at too rapid a pace. Fermentation is the conversion of the sugar contained in the grape into roughly equal parts of alcohol and carbon dioxide. There are vents on the closed white wine tanks to allow the carbon dioxide to escape. Nature's way of allowing grapes to ferment is for the various strains of yeast that grow on the grape skins in the vineyards to develop. But that's rather unpredictable, so we've selected yeast strains that are kept in the laboratories from one harvest, or vintage, to the next. "Vintage wine" is really a misnomer, since vintage refers to the grapes gathered in a given year. Some years are better than others, which has brought about the use of the description of a vintage year. If you want to watch the fermentation process, we can go up on the catwalk overhead and look into the red wine tanks,' Paul offered.

Alisa nodded quickly, growing more intrigued with each moment. She followed Paul along to the stairs, grateful for his steadying hand as they made the steep climb. Walking practically amid the rafters of the building, Alisa was thrilled with her new vantage point. She could look right down into the tanks to see the frothing white foam seething on top of the juice while inhaling the heady scent of fermenting grapes.

'It takes from one to two weeks before the major part of the fermentation is over. In the case of rosé wine they're allowed to ferment with their skins on for only a few hours rather than several days. This is to prevent them from acquiring too much colour from the grape skins,' Paul continued. 'They're drawn off into other casks, leaving the skin sediment behind. When the fermentation process quiets down, the new wine is moved

146

to regular storage tanks or casks.' After allowing her to pause and watch the process, he led her on once again, taking her down the steps to the main floor, then to another building. Here were more enormous tanks, some made of wood and others were shining, gleaming stainless steel. 'Collectively these bulk containers are known as cooperage and come in various sizes and materials ranging from wood to stainless steel to concrete. Each winemaker has his own particular reason for using one instead of another.'

There was a sense of timelessness about this room, Alisa discovered as they wandered slowly in the shadows of the cooperage forest. Here it seemed that time stood still. All was quiet within the walls, waiting with expectant silence. It was a peaceful hush that held the promise of fulfilment.

'So this is where you've carried my wife off too,' Zachary's voice echoed loudly with its mocking tones into the silence.

Paul laughed easily – something he wouldn't have been able to do a few short months ago, Alisa realized. 'Hardly, Zach,' he answered. 'Just revealing to her all the mysteries of wine-making.'

'In that case, there's a call for you from San Francisco. You can take it in my office.' Zachary's long strides quickly brought him abreast of them.

'I got Alisa as far as the cooperage. You can take her on from there,' Paul replied. His blond-brown head turned to Alisa, smiling at her fondly while his eyes roved over her regretfully. 'Zach can explain everything much more ably than I can, anyway.'

'You underrate yourself, Paul,' Alisa said softly,

wishing there was a way she could tell him that she didn't want to be left alone with her husband, especially in this deserted building.

'Still playing around with him, huh, Alisa?' Zachary stated once Paul was out of sight. 'Like a fish on a hook?'

'All we did was go through the winery. What could be more innocent than that?' she retaliated.

'I understand he's been down to the house several times recently,' he persisted.

'On the patio in full view of anyone who wanted to watch.' She glared at him coldly. 'Can the same be said for all your visits from Renée?'

'Always fighting every inch of the way, aren't you?' Zachary smiled with almost disinterested amusement. 'The best defence is a good offence, right?'

'Where you're concerned, yes,' Alisa replied. She turned her back to him and stared firmly at the huge wooden tanks. 'Tell me, how long do the wines stay in these containers?'

'Why are you trying to change the subject?' he laughed. 'Afraid?'

'Yes.'

'I didn't think you would be honest enough to admit it. Are you afraid of me ... or you?' He seemed closer to her than before, even though she had heard no sound of footsteps.

'What an absurd question!' Alisa walked away with a disgusted shrug of her shoulders. 'I'd like to see the rest of the winery. If you're not interested in showing it to me, I'll go up to the office and wait for Paul.'

She turned to see his reaction to her ultimatum. He

was watching with amused thoughtfulness. It was difficult to meet his look, but she did so defiantly.

'Are you really interested in the winery?' he asked.

'After all, it is my husband's business,' she retorted with all the sarcasm she could put into the words.

'That's never concerned you before, so I hardly think it's your reason now. Therefore I must assume you are interested,' indolently disregarding her challenge.

'Now, forgive me if I repeat some of the things Paul has already told you.' Zachary was immediately all business, speaking in clear, concise language that captured Alisa's interest despite her antagonism. 'The wines are held here in cooperage for various lengths of time that are solely dependent on what the end product is to be. Wines that are to be drunk in the full bloom of their youth are bottled after a few months. Other wines that are going to be held for a longer period of ageing are racked or moved from one container to other successively smaller casks. This could mean a time period of over a year to three years.' With a firm grip on Alisa's arm, he guided her to the rear of the cooperage building down a flight of stairs to a cellar. 'There are two reasons for changing wine containers; one is to make the wine clearer with each change and the other is to intensify the changes brought on by ageing. You've already seen where we store some of the bigger casks in the building containing my office. We store a few more down here.' A sweeping hand spread out before her to show more stacks of slightly smaller barrels.

'At the far side,' leading her along as he spoke, 'is

where we stack the cases of already bottled wine, referred to as binning. It used to be that individual bottles were stacked, but it's been found that putting them in cases means there are fewer handlings and better protection from the light. Here again they age for a few weeks, months, or years, depending on the winemaker's wishes.' His eyes dwelled on her attentive features. 'Today wine isn't made strictly for the rich. It's for everyone. With the many different varieties of wine on the market today, there's certain to be a wine that pleases anyone's taste buds. The expensive imported wines are still around to be used as a social symbol for the rich, but more ordinary people in the United States are discovering the pleasure of a glass of inexpensive wine with their meals.'

'Where do you do the bottling?' Alisa asked.

'In another small building behind the office. I can't take you through there today since it's too small. I hope to enlarge it next year,' Zachary replied with a polite but incredibly distant smile. 'There are variations in the making of dessert and sparkling wines, but I'm sure you've seen the basic process today, enough to confuse you without boggling your mind with the solera process for sherries. Now I'll take you back upstairs and point the way to the house.'

'Meaning I've trespassed on your preserve for as long as you'll allow me,' Alisa retorted sharply, jerking away from the hand that sought to help her up the steps.

'Meaning I haven't eaten my lunch, I'm hungry, and I have a great deal of work to do!' This time there was the fire of anger in his eyes. 'And I'm in no mood to bicker with you!'

'The message has been received, sir!' Her eyes glittered coldly under her cynical mask of subservience. 'It's a pity I'm not as easy to handle as Renée.'

'It certainly is.' A fatigued look of boredom crossed his tanned face as he glanced at her briefly.

With a flash of temper, Alisa raced up the steps to the door. Halting long enough at the top for Zachary to point the way, she hurried down the long aisle to another door that led to the outside. Zachary didn't follow her, evidently taking another exit that would lead him to his office. She took several deep breaths in the clear air, determined to check her anger so that no one else would see her loss of composure.

'Hello there! Tour all finished?' Paul called out from where he stood beside his car.

'Yes, yes, it is,' Alisa replied with forced lightness. 'Where are you off to?'

'Nowhere in particular. I was just going to make a few calls on some distributors before going into San Francisco. Is there something you wanted?' he replied as Alisa made her way calmly to his side.

'Nothing special,' she breathed in deeply, glancing over her shoulder in the direction of Zachary's office. 'I was just going to offer you something cold to drink since you've already had lunch.'

'I can spare the time,' he smiled. 'Do you want to ride down, or shall we walk?'

'Let's ride. My feet have done enough walking through the winery,' Alisa laughed, letting her gaze trail over his pleasantly attractive face with the sandy blond hair and blue eyes. She realized she was making a petty attempt at revenge for Zachary's frequently stated desire that she have little to do with Paul, but she didn't care. She wanted to get under Zachary's skin and irritate him the way he irritated her. Also there were a few things she wanted to find out herself, and Paul would be the perfect person to supply the answers.

Once they were settled on the patio with a pitcher filled with lemonade and ice, Alisa kept the conversation on the winery and the different things she had seen. She surprised herself at the way she could manipulate Paul and the situation. She hadn't realized she could be quite so resourceful. Slowly she led the subject around to Renée and the approaching party.

'What do you know about Renée and Zachary?' Alisa asked, adding hastily at Paul's startled expression, 'before we were married, of course.'

'They were together a lot,' Paul replied after a pause to enable him to choose his words carefully. 'I think almost everyone expected them to marry. Especially Renée, which is probably the reason you don't see much of her.'

'Why do you suppose Zachary didn't marry her?' Alisa frowned slightly. 'I guess women are always curious about who their husbands knew before them. But it just seems like their marriage would have suited him perfectly.'

'True. Mr. Gautier made no bones about wanting Zach to take over his vineyards,' Paul agreed, slowly warming to the subject in spite of his reluctance to discuss it with Alisa. 'It's not as if he was trying to palm an ugly daughter off on Zach either. Renée is a very beautiful woman, a little too spoiled in my opinion, but beautiful.'

'I would have thought it was everything Zach would have wanted. I'm sure Mr. Gautier would have given him the money to modernize this vineyard.' Alisa was getting nervous. Again the terrible doubt came up as to the reason Zachary married her. If he could have got all he wanted from the Gautiers, then why did he marry her and insist that it was the money?

'I'm sure he would,' shrugged Paul. 'Still, Zachary is an obstinate man, who very much wants to be in total control of his own destiny. These last couple of years the Stuart Vineyard has been able to make enough of a profit to make its own improvements. Renée is a pretty demanding woman. I imagine Zach decided to enjoy her company without entangling himself with marriage for profit.'

But that was what he had done, Alisa mused silently. Of course, the contract was for only one year with no option for renewal. 'Paul,' she leaned forward, her face earnestly expressing her desire for him to answer her next question, 'how ... how close were they?'

His tanned cheeks darkened with additional colour as he turned away from her gaze. 'I don't imagine Zach had to marry her to get what he wanted that way.' His troubled glance moved back to study her face. 'Alisa, this is past history, something we shouldn't even be discussing. Zach is married to you now. It's all over between him and Renée.'

'What if ... what if I told you it wasn't?' There was a shimmering film of pain in her blue eyes that Alisa wasn't even aware of.

'You can't be serious. Zach would never do that to you. I know he comes on strong, sometimes cruelly hard, but no matter how much running around he's done in the past, I just can't see him doing it when he's married.' With incredulous disbelief Paul reached over and covered Alisa's hand. 'Believe me, Alisa.'

'I wish I could, Paul. It's terribly humiliating to me, thinking that ...' She stopped. She almost sounded jealous, she thought. That was ridiculous. She was just angry that Zachary would carry on like that right under her nose. 'You've seen how often she comes to the winery, Paul. She never stops at the house. She only goes to the winery where Zachary is.'

'Have you talked to him about this?' Paul asked.

'He refuses to discuss it with me.' A hint of her former coldness crept into her voice as she stared down at her hands. 'I needed to talk to someone about it. I have no one else to turn to except you.'

'You know the way I feel about you, Alisa. Nothing's changed in that. I almost wish it were true about Zachary and Renée. If things get too rough for you, you can always call on me, any time, any place.'

'This party, Paul, is it very important?' Alisa asked after smiling her thanks for his offer. 'I mean, I'm not looking forward to going.'

'You'll have to go, Alisa. It would be an enormous insult to the Gautiers if you refused. They invite only a few select people, and to turn down an invitation would be the worst thing that you could do.'

'It was a thought.' If the party was that important Alisa knew Zachary would drag her there by the hair. There was no alternative except to go and try to show up Renée.

'I have to go, Alisa. But remember, you can call me any time.' Paul rose, still holding her hand firmly in his.

'I will, Paul. Thank you for being here,' taking the utmost comfort in looking at the open concern in his blue eyes as they gazed into hers.

CHAPTER EIGHT

ALISA adjusted the full-length gilt edged mirror in its free-standing frame, then stepped back to survey her reflection. After spending nearly an entire day in San Francisco, in and out of the best shops in the city, she had finally found the gown she was looking for to wear to the Gautiers' party tonight. Although she tried to appraise herself critically now, Alisa couldn't keep the glow of triumph from lighting her blue eyes.

It was an original creation, aptly titled 'Pièce de Résistance'. The rich, shimmering midnight blue cloth clung suggestively over her body enhancing the long-limbedness of her legs and accenting her pale golden hair as the midnight sky highlighted the moonlight. But it was the style most of all that had drawn Alisa, daring, sensuous, and elegant all in the same evening gown. Dipping low in the back, the front was a plunging halter opening. The full curve of her breasts was never exposed, yet its existence was accentuated with boldness. Never before had Alisa worn anything that made such a display of her body. But it would certainly overshadow anything Renée would wear, and that was her aim.

From the bed, Alisa picked up the matching three-cornered shawl. Its vee back discreetly concealed the bareness of her skin while the other two corners could be drawn through a beautiful rhinestone ring to conceal the daring plunge in the front. Her shoes were silvery, sparkling delicate heels that dressed the slenderness of her ankle.

Alisa wished that Christine were here to admire the new gown with her. But, rather than impose on Nora to stay in the house with Chris, Alisa had allowed Chris to spend the night with one of her new school friends, and her little sister had been quite content with the decision, looking upon it as a grown-up adventure.

Gathering up her rhinestone-beaded handbag, Alisa cast one last look at her reflection, smoothed the sides of her pale hair where it was swept on top of her head into a sophisticated array of curls. She had heard Zachary leave his room several minutes earlier and knew he must be downstairs waiting for her. He was just closing the door to his den when she made her way slowly down the staircase, feeling his eyes watching her progress but refusing to meet his gaze. When he walked to the bottom step to take her arm, Alisa raised her head coolly towards him, silently admiring the white dinner jacket perfectly tailored to set off the wide shoulders and narrowing waist. He, too, was formidably attractive this evening.

'My wife does me honour this evening.' There was an irritatingly sardonic tone in his voice that for a moment dampened Alisa's pleasure. But the obvious compliment in his dark eyes as he inclined his head towards her soon rose her spirits again.

'You look very stunning yourself,' Alisa returned, a slight lift to her eyebrow as she spoke. 'Are we ready to leave?'

They proceeded out the door to the car in silence. It wasn't until Zachary had pulled out of the lane on to the main road that he initiated further conversation.

'This won't be an ordinary cocktail party. The guests will be fellow vintners like myself and their families, who over the years have become close friends with Louis Gautier. Only wine will be served,' Zachary explained quietly, his eyes leaving the road only occasionally to glance at Alisa to make sure she was listening to him. 'And then probably only champagne. It's a very important tradition in the Gautier family, one that's been carried down from the first harvest season. It's both a solemn and a festive celebration. I would hope you'll treat it as such and not indulge in any scenes.'

'I wouldn't dream of it,' Alisa smiled easily. 'But I do hope our host's daughter agrees with you.'

'I wouldn't worry about Renée,' Zachary said grimly.

Alisa would have liked to make an appropriate retort, but they had already reached their destination. One glance at the imposing house told Alisa that if she had thought Zachary's home resembled a comfortable country estate, this was truly a mansion. The low rambling, red-tiled roof meandered over a wide-spreading home; the immaculate lawn was a landscaper's dream; the whole effect was one of continuous affluence. Zachary parked their car in a large paved parking lot already half filled with other cars of people who had already arrived. There seemed no further need for conversation as they walked the short distance from the car to the ornately carved doors of the main entrance. The door was opened almost the instant they reached it. A uniformed servant ushered them into a large room filled with expensive Louis XIV furniture and priceless antiques. Their host and hostess were just inside the door welcoming their guests as they arrived.

'Zachary, how good of you to come,' Louis Gautier greeted him happily, grasping Zachary's hand and shaking it enthusiastically.

'You know we wouldn't have missed your celebration. It's as much a part of the vintage season as the grapes,' Zachary replied, inclining his head deferentially.

'Mrs. Stuart,' Louis turned his head to welcome Alisa, taking her hand to touch it lightly with his lips in a continental salute. 'How exquisitely lovely you look this evening. Your dress is the colour of my Pinot Noir grapes when they reflect the velvety hue of our clear blue skies. The very grapes from which I make my champagne wine.'

'I'm flattered,' Alisa murmured, warmed by this gallant and charming man.

'Let us hope my champagne turns out to be as alluring and as temptingly delicious as your gown,' Louis bowed in return.

'I'm sure, Louis,' Zachary broke in, his hand resting lightly on the shawl covering Alisa's back, 'that you're overrating my wife's gown and underrating your wine.'

'I would prefer that they both be the *pièce de résistance*,' Louis replied with courtly politeness. 'Would you care to remove your wrap, Mrs. Stuart?'

'What a coincidence that you should use that phrase,' Alisa remarked, removing the rhinestone ring that held the shawl in place. 'That is the exact name of this creation.'

A sparkling light gleamed admiringly from the older man's eyes as the blue shawl slipped down on Alisa's shoulders. There was a barely perceptible sound to her left which brought her gaze to it. Renée, regally resplendent in a red velvet gown, was staring at her with open hatred. A haughty, triumphant glance touched fleetingly the corners of Alisa's mouth as she boldly met the malevolent stare.

'I believe it's you, Zachary, who have underestimated your wife,' Louis said quietly, drawing her attention to the man towering over her on her right side.

'Perhaps I have,' Zachary stared down at her, his eyes masked in a light that was blacker than his dark hair and impossible to read.

Another group of guests arrived and Zachary and Alisa wandered into the room. Strangely, Renée was nowhere to be seen. Alisa realized her victory had been only in a minor skirmish and the rest of the evening stretched ahead of her. She had expected Zachary to make some comment about her gown, but he never referred to it. Except during introductions to various couples, he hardly even glanced at her, which was difficult to understand. Only the admiring looks from the male members of the party assured Alisa that her gown was vastly becoming even though her own husband seemed unmoved by its daring décolleté.

The soft melody played by an accomplished string quartet located in the far corner of the room came to an end. There was a brief hush in the crowd as Louis Gautier walked to the centre of the room. With an aristocratic assurance that was accented by his distinguished appearance, he paused for their undivided attention. Then he lifted a tulip-shaped glass in front of him. It was an obvious signal, for almost immediately a group of dark-suited waiters appeared carrying trays of similar glasses that were passed around to the guests.

'Ladies and gentlemen.' His resonant voice didn't raise an octave, still it carried to the farthest corner of the room. 'Tonight marks the end of another vintage, the success of which we have come to celebrate. The cultivation of wine grapes began in California two hundred years ago by Spanish missionaries. Since that time, the vineyards and wineries have combated disease, the uncertainties of Mother Nature, and the Congress in Washington, D.C. with their law of Prohibition.' There were quiet chuckles and nodding smiles at his statement. 'But we withstood them all, we *vignerons* and the grape. Today we compete with the very best wines all over the world. Let us lift our glasses this night to the time when our sparkling California champagne captures the delicacy typical of its European namesake.' There was a tinkling of glasses as all raised theirs in salute. 'To our California wine,' Louis toasted proudly.

'That is a concession that is only made in the presence of fellow vintners,' Paul whispered from behind Alisa. 'In public, no one will admit that our California wine is not as good or better than those from Europe.'

The effervescent liquid tingled down her throat as Alisa turned to greet Paul. Zachary watched with indulgent aloofness as if assured that he had no reason for concern that Paul was a rival. His indifference irked

Alisa and she turned her most charming skills on Paul.

'I was looking for you, but I didn't see you come in,' Her eyes seemed a deeper blue with the reflection from her shimmering gown.

'I saw you the minute I entered the room,' Paul answered, his eyes devouring her appearance. 'You look absolutely ravishing this evening.'

One of Zachary's acquaintances came up to claim his attention, though he still watched Alisa with amusement dancing in his eyes.

'What do you think of the little gathering?' Paul asked.

'Terribly formal, isn't it?' Alisa laughed, glancing around at the richly gowned women and the elegantly groomed men.

'Winemaking is an extremely traditional and serious business,' he smiled, following her glance around the room. 'Notice the men. See how they swirl the wine in their glass, sniffing the bouquet before they allow the liquid to touch their mouth, studying the colour obtrusively in the light. Only the very best of the Gautier champange is served tonight. This is a group of true connoisseurs gathering to pay homage to one of their peers.'

Alisa was barely listening to him. She was watching Renée slowly wending her way through the crowd in their direction or more correctly in Zachary's direction. Her arms curled possessively around his left arm as she edged herself between Zachary and Alisa, her face upturning provocatively towards his as she murmured her greeting. Alisa watched in almost furious silence as

Zachary gazed down at Renée, his eyes travelling admiringly over her gown and face. Their interchange was spoken so softly that Alisa couldn't hear what was being said. The man previously talking to Zachary moved discreetly away, which irritated Alisa even further. At last, Renée fluttered a hand up to his cheek before releasing her hold on his arm and making a swirling turn away from him. She met Alisa's gaze for a brief moment, her dark eyes flashing with an unmistakable challenge.

'Don't let her get to you,' Paul prompted from her side.

Alisa turned with a start, then smiled apologetically at the diversion of her attention. 'I try not to,' she sighed.

'Try not to what?' Zachary asked, mockingly meeting her frigid glance. 'I noticed you didn't say hello to our host's daughter.'

'I notice she didn't say hello to me,' she answered sharply. 'But then she was too busy gazing into my husband's eyes to see me, wasn't she?'

'Was she? I didn't notice,' Zachary answered, calmly sipping from his glass.

Paul glanced uncomfortably from one to the other, while Alisa took a larger gulp from her glass.

'I wouldn't drink the champagne quite so quickly,' Zachary advised quietly. 'It's likely to go to your head.'

Rebelliously Alisa drained the glass and motioned to one of the waiters for another which he quickly supplied. Her hand trembled slightly with her anger as she held the new glass stiffly in her hand.

'Zachary!' Renée called gaily, moving quickly through the crowd to where the trio stood. 'Papa said we could begin dancing now.' Her voice carried clearly over the drone of conversation from the other guests. 'I have chosen you to be my first partner.'

'With your permission,' Zachary inclined his head towards Alisa, the wickedly mocking smile tugging at the corners of his mouth.

'And if I refuse?' She spoke in a voice just loud enough for him to hear.

'Then you would be creating a scene.' There was a slight underscoring of the word 'you' as he answered in the same quiet voice.

Alisa was left with no choice except to nod her permission for Zachary to partner Renée. But she refused to meet the triumphant glitter in Renée's eyes, choosing instead to turn towards Paul and smile as if nothing at all was wrong. Try as she would, though, Alisa couldn't keep her gaze from straying to the dance floor where the couple danced exceedingly close together, their feet moving slowly around the floor. When the song ended, Zachary didn't return to her side. Instead he squired other female guests on to the dance floor, never once approaching Alisa. Twice she danced with Paul, smiling with false sweetness at Zachary when they neared him and his partner on the floor.

Alisa had finished another glass of champagne and was just about to light a cigarette when her host walked up to ask her to dance. Zachary was on the floor again – with Renée. Alisa quickly accepted Louis Gautier's invitation, discovering he was an extremely accomplished dancer whose fluid movements easily matched with hers. There was a great deal of applause for them from the guests when the song ended. Louis had just insisted on repeating the dance when Zachary tapped him lightly on the shoulder.

'I haven't had the privilege of dancing with my wife yet this evening, Louis. Do you mind?'

Louis sighed expressively before bowing formally to Alisa and stepping away.

'I didn't think you'd noticed,' Alisa declared sarcastically as Zachary's hand touched the bare skin of her back. 'Or was it a case of pleasure before duty?'

'You catch more bees with honey than vinegar,' Zachary replied, taking her hand in a vice-like grip as he firmly guided her to match his steps.

'But then who would want to be stung by a bee?' Alisa said sharply. She was irritatingly aware that he held her apart from him. There was none of the intimate closeness of touching bodies when he danced with her. Even when avoiding another couple on the floor, he managed to do so without drawing Alisa closer to him.

'With some people, the bee doesn't sting.'

'Like Renée?' Alisa asked.

'Renée could be one.' Zachary smiled mysteriously at her, his gaze roving almost indifferently over her face.

'You didn't mention whether you liked my gown,' Alisa went on, nodding towards Louis, who was dancing with his wife.

'Didn't I? It's very nice. A little daring for you, though,' Zachary jeered, taking amusement at the quick flash of anger in her eyes.

'How would you know?' she retorted, just as the song ended. She would have walked away except that his hand still maintained its hold on hers. He solemnly escorted her to the edge of the dance floor where Paul was standing.

'You've been quite determined to keep me at arms' length, remember, Alisa,' Zachary smiled.

He nodded towards Paul, then moved off to claim Mrs. Gautier for the next dance. Alisa walked away from the floor with Paul following anxiously behind her. A waiter offered her a glass of champagne which she accepted. Paul offered her a cigarette, lit it for her, and watched while she puffed it angrily.

'Alisa . . .' he began hesitantly.

'I will not be treated like this!' she exclaimed, her angry eyes glaring back at the dance floor to see Renée breaking in on Zachary and her mother. 'I will not be some piece of baggage that can be set aside whenever he chooses and remembered when he feels it's his duty!'

'Alisa—' Paul said soothingly.

'Look at how he dances with her!' She attempted to lower her voice, although she didn't hide the venom. 'They're almost making love right there on the floor!'

'Hardly that,' Paul protested, at his wits' end as to how to cope with her.

'I'm not staying here another minute.' She snubbed her cigarette out haphazardly in a nearby ashtray. 'Paul, will you take me home?'

'You can't leave. It would look terrible if you left without Zachary.'

'Would it? How inconvenient for him,' Alisa sneered, swallowing the last of the liquid from her glass, handing it to a nearby waiter.

'Alisa, be reasonable.'

'I am being reasonable. Now either you take me home or I'll walk.'

'I'll take you,' Paul sighed reluctantly.

He went to get the car while Alisa waited for one of the servants to bring her shawl. She paced restlessly in the hall, half afraid that Zachary would appear and stop her and half hoping that he would try. But only Mrs. Gautier appeared, concerned that Alisa was leaving so early.

'I have such a wretched headache,' Alisa lied, 'that, as much as I've enjoyed your party, just won't go away.'

Mrs. Gautier accepted the explanation, agreeing to pass on Alisa's gratitude for the invitation to her husband. Alisa was relieved to see the servant arrive with her shawl. She said her good-byes quickly, repeating her gratitude, then hurried out the door to Paul's car.

'Are you sure you don't want to change your mind, Alisa?' Paul asked as he shifted the gears out of neutral. 'I'm sure it isn't all as bad as it seems. After all, Zachary has to be polite to Renée.'

'I didn't see you dancing with her,' Alisa replied, fighting the slight wave of lightheadedness that had assaulted her upon entering the outdoors. Paul smiled a little sheepishly. 'I don't want to talk about it.'

She emphasized her request by turning to stare out the window at the star-filled sky. Paul accepted her edict with silence, glancing at her still figure silhouetted by the pale moonlight. She was so confused, her thoughts filled chaotically with anger, self-pity, indignation and resignation. Her emotions were so churned up inside her that she didn't know exactly what she was feeling except there was a pain lodged in her throat that made speaking almost impossible. When the wheels of the car rolled to a halt on the crunching gravel driveway of her home, Alisa stared at it absently. It seemed so long ago that Zachary had brought her and Christine here. The future had looked so entirely different then. She had thought she could cope with anything, but she couldn't begin to cope with Zachary. He had blocked her at every turn.

Paul got out of the car and walked around to open her door. 'Do you want me to walk you to the door?' he asked.

'No,' she answered shortly, fighting the constriction in her throat.

Taking the hand he offered, she stepped on to the sidewalk. He held her hand to keep her beside him, gazing helplessly into her face. She would have liked to reassure him that everything was going to be all right, but she didn't believe it herself.

'Alisa.' Paul breathed her name in a caress, pulling her into his arms where he held her tightly against him. 'I wish there was something I could do or say.' She made a protesting little move in his arms that brought his hand to her chin. Gently he tilted it level with his, leaning forward to touch her lips in a soothing, controlled kiss. Then almost regretfully he released her, standing aside while she walked slowly towards the house. She turned once to wave to him and watched from the doorway as he drove away before she closed the door and entered the large foyer. The shawl, hung heavily on her shoulders, so she pulled it off, and tossed it on the bureau. The click of her heels echoed loudly in the empty house as Alisa walked across the hall into the living-room, her arms hugged about her tightly to ward off the chill that seemed to be creeping through her.

'That was a very short good night scene.'

Alisa's head lifted sharply to see Zachary seated in one of the armchairs in the darkened room.

'How did you get here?' she gasped.

'As soon as I learned my wife wasn't feeling well, I took the short cut through the vineyards,' he answered calmly, rising to walk towards her.

'I suppose you're angry,' Alisa sighed, suddenly not caring whether he was or not.

'At you leaving the party without telling me? Or for kissing Paul just a minute ago?'

'For both, I suppose,' Alisa answered.

'The first offered me a good excuse to leave the party myself.' His eyes mocked her glance of surprise. 'And the second reminded me how inexperienced you are at making love.'

'The kiss meant nothing,' she shrugged.

'Every kiss means something. I think it's time I showed you what I'm talking about. There are all kinds of kisses, each with a different purpose.'

Alisa was confused. She hadn't expected this kind of reaction from Zachary. Even as his hands moved to rest on her arms, the very lightness of his hold made moving away from him a ridiculously childish gesture. Instead she turned her face up to him, curious to discover what he was going to do.

'First of all, there's the duty kiss, much like the one you gave me on our wedding day.' His lips brushed hers lightly, a surprising coolness in the touch. 'Then there's a kiss between two friends.' Again the touch was light, but this time there seemed a bit of warmth to it. He didn't seem to be expecting any resistance from Alisa and she wasn't giving any. 'Of course, we have the gentle good night kiss, too.' As his lips descended again on hers, there was a slight pressure that Alisa found pleasing. The slowness with which his lips left hers left a feeling of regret behind.

'The next kiss is, I imagine, the type of kiss that Paul gave you, that of a person in love, but who mustn't show it.' His hands left her shoulders and moved to her back where he could pull her into his arms, kissing her easily, but without any marked ardency. It was much like the way Paul had kissed her except that she didn't feel the same way, so it couldn't have been the champagne. Something was happening and Alisa wasn't sure she liked it. As he released her, she tried to pull away. 'Not yet,' he reproached her softly. 'There's one more. Surely you can resist one more?'

'This . . . this is silly,' Alisa stammered.

'One more.' His coaxing tone weakened her defences that had already been eroded by the champagne. 'The kiss that a man gives to a woman he loves.' There was only the very slightest amount of resistance in Alisa as he drew her slowly into his arms. She watched the sensuous curve of his mouth as it lowered towards hers. A flash of exquisite sweetness seared through her at the incredible persuasive ardour in the kiss, her own lips parting almost of their own volition. At this tiny spark of response, Zachary's arms tightened their hold about her, his hands moving down to the small of her back, arching her against him. She tried to remember that she shouldn't respond, that she shouldn't show him that for the first time in her life she was enjoying being kissed, that she felt no feeling of repugnance in his embrace. But it was no use. Her fingers curled around the lapel of his coat as he increased the passion in his kiss and she answered it with her own. Almost reluctantly, his lips left hers even though she involuntarily moved forward to try to recapture them again.

She stared up to his face, barely visible in the waning light. There was no mistaking the fiery passion burning in his eyes as he looked down upon her. An inner trembling was coursing through her and her heart was pounding faster than its normal rate. Through his suit she could feel the quickened pace of his heart. A tremulous thrill grew inside her that he had reacted to her as well.

'Is that all?' Her voice came out all husky and thick and he smiled at the sound of it.

He shook his head negatively to the side. 'When a man wants to make love to a woman, he sometimes kisses her like this.'

Love – love: Her mind reeled. Why did he keep using that word? This time there was no initial gentleness when his mouth descended on hers. Immediately Alisa was overwhelmed by the demanding, taking power in his kiss. But she was more frightened by the strange feeling that was taking over her own body, the growing heat in her own loins that was spreading its warmth through her limbs until she seemed deprived of any strength to do anything but succumb to whatever he wanted.

'There could only be one reason for this,' her mind cried out. 'You're in love with him.'

'Yes, yes, I am,' her heart replied, as she gave herself up ecstatically to his kiss.

It didn't matter how much she had scoffed at love before. She had never known what it felt like, that it could bring such a wondrous joy and happiness with it. Her arms slid around his neck as she stood on tiptoes, crushed against his body and loving every part of him that touched her. Abruptly he broke away from her lips, his chest rising and falling heavily.

'Zach, Zach,' Alisa murmured, burying her head in his coat, shy and afraid to meet his eyes after baring her feelings so openly in her response to his embrace.

'You learn very quickly. This isn't the champagne, is it?' Alisa made a small negative move of her head. His hand became entangled in her hair as he forced her to look up to him. She gazed at him in open adoration. 'I knew when I saw you in that dress that I wanted to hold you like this.' He inhaled deeply at the look in her eyes. 'You shouldn't look at a man like that, Alisa. It would lead him to think things.'

'I didn't know ... I didn't know it could be like this,' she whispered. Her arms tightened around his neck.

Zachary moaned softly before he covered her mouth with his, forsaking it to rain kisses over her eyes, nose, ears, and neck before coming again to claim her lips. At the same time his hands were moving over the bare skin of her back as if trying to find a way to mould her even closer to his body, the aching need of both of them trying to transcend the limits of physical ability. As his hand moved between them, slipping into the neckline of her gown to cup her rounded, straining breast, Alisa emitted a gasp of fear and pleasure. Almost immediately his hand moved away as his mouth slowly left hers.

'No!' she protested weakly.

Zachary inhaled deeply, 'Alisa, you don't know what you're doing. We either stop now or—' He left the obvious hanging in the air.

'I know,' surprising herself with her own calmness, even as she reached up to touch his lips with her own.

In one movement, he covered her lips and swept her off her feet into his arms. He had carried her to the stairs and his foot was on the first step when the phone rang shrilly. Zachary gazed down at her, his lips touching the arm that encircled his neck.

'Shall we let it ring?' he asked.

Alisa hesitated. 'It might be Chris. Something could have happened.'

He sighed with a reluctance that sent Alisa's heart pounding wilder than before. In the light of her love she understood so many things about their relationship in the past and her unaccountable dislike of Renée.

173

'I wish I'd torn the damn thing off the wall,' Zachary muttered, setting Alisa reluctantly on her feet.

'I'll get it,' she smiled, so happy that he felt as sorry as she did.

His head bent to touch her lips sweetly before she hurried to the hall phone and picked up the receiver, her eyes returning to stare admiringly at this tall, handsome man who was her husband, and whom she loved now so deeply.

'Stuart residence,' she said into the receiver.

'I'd like to speak to Zachary, please,' Renée's voice demanded.

Alisa's heart stopped cold. She began swallowing convulsively as she tried to answer. A wave of cold shame washed over her as she realized that never once had Zachary said he loved her. How often had she drummed it into her own head that men don't have to be in love to make love!

'Alisa, what's wrong?' At the stricken look on Alisa's face, he walked swiftly to her side. 'Who is it?'

'Renée.' The word was practically torn from her throat. 'I suppose you forgot . . .' The hurt was so excruciatingly painful that she could hardly talk. Zachary seemed to sway in front of her in the misty tears that were blocking her vision. '. . . Another rendezvous.'

In the next second she was shoving the receiver into his stunned hand and racing up the stairs to her room. She heard his strident order to come back, but she ignored it. When she heard him direct his words to the phone, her flight to escape increased its pace. Not until she reached her room did Alisa pause, leaning against the closed door, her head moving from side to side in the agony of her shame. She wanted him; she loved him; and she wanted him still, even knowing he was unfaithful, even knowing that he might never be faithful. That was her shame, her humiliation. But she knew, no matter how much she wanted him, she could never do it without love.

Her hands fumbled at the door-knob. There was no lock! In a matter of minutes, Zachary would be coming up the stairs. And there was no way to lock the door! She glanced around the darkened room until her gaze stopped on the straight-backed chair in the corner. Swiftly Alisa raced across the room, bringing it back and propping it under the handle of the door. From the hallway came the sounds of his sure strides. Slowly she backed away from the door, unknowingly holding her breath as he came closer. Her back touched the wall beside the window where she stopped. Her gaze was hypnotized to the door knob.

'Alisa?' The golden knob turned, releasing its catch while the door moved a fraction of an inch before it was held by the chair. 'Alisa!' Zachary's voice was angry and demanding as his fist pounded on the door. 'Open this door!'

She bit her lip to keep from crying out. She wasn't going to answer him.

'Alisa, I want to talk to you.' He made an attempt to control the anger in his voice. 'Renée called to make sure everything was all right. I never had any intention or plan to meet her tonight.'

'Sure,' Alisa thought bitterly, 'she just wanted to make sure everything was all right. Then why didn't she ask me?' she cried out silently.

'Alisa, open the door!'

Zachary was angry. 'Let him be angry,' her heart cried. 'Let him feel the disappointment that I feel!' What would he do? she wondered. Would he break down the door? With the chair that would be practically impossible. There were several more minutes of silence until she finally heard his muffled swearing and his footsteps moving away from the door. Slowly, with every muscle, fibre and bone in her body aching with pain, Alisa turned to stare out the window. She longed for the release that tears would bring, but there was none. She curled her arms about her waist, rocking slowly from side to side trying to comfort the hurt that was too deep to be comforted.

There was a click and the room was illuminated with light. Spinning around, Alisa saw Zachary standing in the room near the doorway to the bathroom that connected her room to Christine's. She had forgotten. So foolishly she had forgotten. Her pain-filled eyes stared into the black fury that covered his face.

'Wouldn't it have been much simpler if you'd just opened the door?' Zachary asked sarcastically.

Her eyes closed briefly as she turned her back to him to stare out the window.

'Damn it, why won't you talk to me? I can explain if you'd give me the chance!' His long, lithe strides carried him swiftly to her.

'Get out of here, Zachary.' Her words came out with all the frigid coldness of her former self.

'And forget what happened downstairs?' His question mocked her more effectively than his voice.

'Mark it up to champagne and moonlight,' Alisa said bitterly. 'After all, what's a few wasted moments?'

'That was real. That happened. I won't accept—' His hands reached out and captured her shoulders. With surprising violence she wrenched herself away from him.

'Don't touch me! Don't ever touch me!' All her control was lost.

Zachary stared down at her, the angry fire in his eyes meeting the blue sparks of hers. For a moment she thought he was going to hit her and she almost welcomed the thought of physical abuse, but it was not to be. Instead he pivoted on his heel and stalked to the door. He stood in front of the chair that had previously barred his entry before picking it up and turning towards Alisa.

'You won't need this tonight.' His jeering voice, a combination of anger and sarcasm. Then he flung the chair across the room as if it was a toothpick before slamming out the door.

The resounding crash of the wooden chair against the wall sounded like an explosion in the room. Alisa's hands covered her ears at the splintering sound. A shudder quaked through her body as she surveyed the damaged chair and wall. Then, almost staggering to the bed, she collapsed on the coverlet, all her energy drained and her spirit dead. In a trance-like state she heard Zachary leave the house. She didn't even spare a thought to where he might be going. He was going to Renée. A convulsion of jealousy stabbed at her body knowing that he could have been there with her.

It was nearly dawn when sleep finally claimed her, carrying her off into a nightmare world where Zachary kept moving out of her reach.

CHAPTER NINE

ALISA gazed out of her window. The noonday sun shone brightly on the autumn colours of red and gold. The rays danced in the window, picking up the shimmer of the stone on her left hand until it appeared as red as the blood that was surely pouring from her broken heart. The light of the new day didn't bring any fresh perspective on her situation. After awaking at nearly ten and making sure that Zachary wasn't in the house, Alisa had gone downstairs, sipped indifferently at her coffee, and tried to think of a logical solution. But her heart wasn't ruled by logic. There only seemed to be one choice.

Sighing heavily, she turned from her bedroom window and walked to the cupboard. From the far corner, she brought out her suitcases. There was no longer any way that she could stay in the same house with Zachary. An annulment would be a simple procedure, one that she would start in motion the minute she left the house. With leaden movements, Alisa opened the suitcases on her bed and began transferring the clothes from her drawers into the empty bags. Outside the closed window she heard a car crunch to a stop, the sound of slamming car doors followed by the opening and closing of the front door of the house. In her lethargic state, her mind registered little else except that it wasn't Zachary's footsteps she heard on the stairs. It really wasn't until Christine came bursting into the room that Alisa had even given a thought to the fact that it wasn't a schoolday.

'Hi! I had a great time. Was the party fun?' The excited voice stopped and the exuberant steps slowed as Christine saw Alisa meticulously folding clothes into the suitcases. 'Where are you going?'

'We're going on a little trip,' Alisa answered calmly. 'What did you and Mary Ann do last night?'

'Nothing really,' Chris answered absently. Her wonderful time faded with this sudden turnabout of affairs. 'Where are we going to go?'

'Oh, we'll probably go see your cousin Michael.' Alisa tried to smile confidently as if it was really going to be an enjoyable time.

The brown eyes inspected Alisa closely, too intense for Alisa to meet the gaze squarely. The small hand trailed idly over the railing at the foot of the bed, as Chris wandered to the opposite side. Then she saw the chair sitting in the corner, its broken leg crumpled beneath it. Seconds later she saw the wall where the plaster had been gouged out.

'What happened to the chair? And the wall?'

Alisa hesitated nervously, her hand crushing the slip in her hand. 'It got broken,' she replied casually.

'Who broke it? Did you?'

'No, I didn't.'

'Then who did? Did Zachary?' Chris persisted.

'Yes.' Alisa slammed the dresser drawer shut harder than she intended.

'This trip we're going to take – when it's over, are we going to come back here?'

Alisa tried desperately to meet the troubled expression on her sister's face. 'Really, Chris,' she laughed, 'you ask so many questions!'

'We're not coming back, are we?' The small face crumpled with her cry. 'We're not ever going to come back!'

'Chris dear, it's so hard to explain.' The lump was back in Alisa's throat, but the child didn't wait for explanations as she ran sobbing out of the room.

For a moment Alisa started to follow her before deciding that it would be best for Chris to be alone, to cry out the hurt as she had not been able to do. She turned back to her packing, trying to block out the accusing look in her sister's face. Angry screams from downstairs halted her. She dropped the clothes in her hand on to the floor and dashed out of the room to the head of the stairs. At the base of the staircase, Christine was screaming and kicking at Zachary, her arms flailing at him ineffectually.

'I hate you! I hate you!' Her cry was a sobbing scream. 'You broke Lisa's chair! I hate you!'

'Christine, stop that at once!' Alisa called sharply, hurrying down the stairs.

'What have you told this child?' Zachary glared accusingly at Alisa now that Christine's attack had begun to subside.

'You broke her chair,' Chris sobbed, 'and now we have to leave. And we're never going to come back!' Her face twisted with pain was turned on Alisa. 'I know it. We're never coming back!'

'You are not leaving, Chris,' said Zachary, his eyes holding Alisa's gaze firmly. When Chris started to protest, he interrupted, 'I don't care what your sister says, you are not leaving. Now go outside, so I can talk to her in private.'

Christine glanced hesitantly towards Alisa, who nodded for her to obey. She hadn't intended to confront Zachary with her decision to leave. She had hoped to leave him a note – a coward's way, she realized, but the easiest way. Now that was denied her. Alisa tried to regard him in a detached way. Although it was difficult, she succeeded.

'Lets' go into the den.' The tight rein on his temper was evident in the way he tried to speak calmly, even though the anger danced in his eyes.

'There's nothing to discuss,' Alisa said coldly.

'You have a choice, Alisa. We can stand here in the hallway and discuss your "nothing" or we can go into the den and do it in private. Make up your mind.' His ultimatum was clear, and stiffly she agreed. He took her arm as if adding ensurance that she would accompany him. Once inside the room with the doors closed behind them, he released her arm and stepped away. He lit a cigarette, offered her one, and put them away when she declined. The silence lengthened unbearably.

'Why are you leaving?' Zachary finally spoke.

'That's a stupid question,' Alisa answered.

'No, it isn't. I want to know why.'

'Because I'm not going to spend another minute in this house,' pausing for effect, 'with you!'

'I won't let you leave.'

'If it's the money you're worried about, you don't have to. The money was yours the day you married me. That was your condition, remember?' Alisa said bitterly.

'I thought you'd bring that up.' Zachary walked to the desk, opened a drawer, removed a small book from it and tossed it to her. 'There's your money, all two hundred thousand. I never touched a penny. I never needed to touch a penny. I'm not rich, but I am self-sufficient.'

Alisa stared at the figures inside the book in dumbfounded silence. 'I don't understand.' She replaced it on his desk as though it was too hot to touch. 'It doesn't change a thing. I'm leaving.'

'Last night, I told Renée I didn't ever want to see her again. I haven't wanted to for a long time, if I ever really did.' Zachary took a step towards her.

'How foolish of you to burn your bridges behind you,' Alisa retorted, turning to leave the room, finding the conversation was more than she could bear.

But Zachary grabbed her by the shoulders and twisted her violently around to face him. Alisa couldn't help cringing at the rage etched on his face. He gave her a short vicious shake.

'Have you forgotten the reason you married me in the first place?' he snarled. 'It was so you could have Chris. You told me your mother's will stated that you had to reside with your husband for one year. You still have a little over eight months to go.'

'You wouldn't,' Alisa gasped. 'I know you care a little bit for her. What goes on between you and me has no bearing on Chris! You wouldn't tell Marguerite?'

'Wouldn't I?' He released her, walked to the desk and picked up the telephone receiver. There was a pause as Zachary dialled. 'Operator, put me through to the Roy Denton residence in Oakland, California ... No, I don't know the number.'

Alisa stared at him in disbelief. His dark eyes jeered her from her frozen immobility. His mouth curved wickedly as she tore the receiver from his hand and slammed it back on its rest.

'How can you be so cruel? How can you do this?' she sobbed.

'I won't let you go. Alisa.' She could no longer doubt that he meant it. The hard, uncompromising expression on his face made it unbelievably clear.

'Why? Why?' Her voice was a mere whisper.

Zachary reached out, gripping her shoulders so tightly that she moaned unwillingly at the pain. He crushed her against him, his hand forcing his head against his chest.

'Because I'm a fool,' he growled. His hand roughly stroked her head. 'Because I need you. Because last night I saw all the cold reserve leave you and you became a woman – my woman, Alisa. I'll make you mine again.'

'Please,' she begged, pushing weakly against him in an effort to free herself. 'Don't humiliate me any more. Isn't it enough that you made me love you? Must you take away my pride and self-respect. too?'

'You do love me.' He pinioned her face between his hands. The passion and desire filled his eyes as he greedily inspected every curve and angle of her face. 'I don't want to take away your pride, my darling,' he murmured. At the startled and surprised expression in her eyes, he laughed softly. 'My beautiful wife, you believe that I merely wanted to possess you last night. I did, make no mistake about that. But because I love you! I need you because I love you!'

He leaned forward to kiss her lips, but Alisa stepped away, not willing to believe what he was saying.

'Please, Zachary, don't play with me. Don't use me.' She stepped away again as he moved towards her. The glint in his eyes became harder to resist. She put up a hand to ward him off. 'Why did you marry me?'

'I had no intention of marrying you,' Zachary smiled. 'That night in the casino I went along with you to see how far you would go, to see just how much you would do to get your sister.' At her indrawn breath, Zachary looked at her tenderly. 'You must remember that I knew how callously cruel you'd been to Paul. But the following morning when I went to tell you what I thought of you, I saw you all soft and tousled by sleep, looking so vulnerable and alone, and I knew I was going to marry you. I told myself that I would make you fall in love with me so you would know some of the pain that Paul went through, never knowing that I would go through it myself. I must have fallen in love with you that morning.'

This time she didn't resist when he took her in his arms, murmuring over and over again how much she loved him, but her words were constantly being silenced by his kisses. A small sound from the doorway brought Zachary's head up, though he didn't loosen his loving hold on Alisa.

'Are we leaving?' Chris asked hesitantly from the door.

'No,' Alisa answered softly, gazing adoringly into Zachary's face.

'Maybe for a few days, as a sort of belated honeymoon,' Zachary corrected her before turning to the auburn-haired child at the door. 'Come here, Peanut,' affectionately gathering Christine into an arm and lifting her up so that all three were encircled in the same embrace. 'We're a family now.'

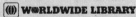

Harlequin "Super Celebration" SWEEPSTAKES

NEW PRIZES—NEW PRIZE FEATURES & CHOICES—MONTHLY

1. To enter the sweepstakes, follow the instructions outlined on the Center Insert Card. Alternate means of entry, NO PURCHASE NECESSARY, you may also enter by mailing your name, address and birthday on a plain 3" x 5" piece of paper to: In U.S.A.: Harlequin "Super Celebration" Sweepstakes, P.O. Box 1867, Buffalo, N.Y. 14240-1867. In Canada: Harlequin "Super Celebration" Sweepstakes, P.O. Box 2800, 5170 Yonge Street, Postal Station A, Willowdale, Ontario M2N 6J3.

2. Winners will be selected in random drawings from all entries received. All prizes will be awarded. These prizes are in addition to any free gifts which might be offered. Versions of this sweepstakes with different prizes may appear in other presentations by TorStar and their affiliates. The maximum value of the prizes offered is $8,000.00. Winners selected will receive the prize offered from their prize package.

3. The selection of winners will be conducted under the supervision of Marden-Kane, an independent judging organization. By entering the sweepstakes, each entrant accepts and agrees to be bound by these rules and the decision of the judges which shall be final and binding. Odds of winning are dependent upon the total number of entries received. Taxes, if any, are the sole responsibility of the winners. Prizes are not transferable. This sweepstakes is scheduled to appear in Retail Outlets of Harlequin Books during the period of June 1986 to December 1986. All entries must be received by January 31st, 1987. The drawing will take place on or about March 1st, 1987 at the offices of Marden-Kane, Lake Success, New York. For Quebec (Canada) residents, any litigation regarding the running of this sweepstakes and the awarding of prizes must be submitted to La Regie de Lotteries et Course du Quebec.

4. This presentation offers the prizes as illustrated on the Center Insert Card.

5. This offer is open to residents of the U.S., and Canada, 18 years or older, except employees of TorStar, its affiliates, subsidiaries, Marden-Kane and all other agencies and persons connected with conducting this sweepstakes. All Federal, State and local laws apply. Void where prohibited or restricted by law. Winners will be notified by mail and may be required to execute an affidavit of eligibility and release which must be returned within 14 days after notification. Winners consent to the use of their name, photograph and/or likeness for advertising and publicity in conjunction with this and similar promotions without additional compensation. One prize per family or household. Canadian winners will be required to answer a skill testing question.

6. For a list of our most recent prize winners, send a stamped, self-addressed envelope to: WINNERS LIST, c/o Marden-Kane, P.O. Box 525, Sayreville, NJ 08872.

No Lucky Number needed to win!

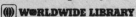

HARLEQUIN HISTORICAL

Explore love with Harlequin in the Middle Ages, the Renaissance, in the Regency, the Victorian and other eras.

Relive within these books the endless ages of romance, set against authentic historical backgrounds. Two new historical love stories published each month.